Back on Top
A Celebrity Spin Doctor Novel
Celia Mulder

Cats in Libraries Press

Book Cover by Najla Qamber

Edited by Aubrey Bobak

2nd edition 2025

DEDICATION

To Ocean's 6, BTS, and Blake Lively's pantsuits for sticking with me through this wacky series.

CONTENTS

CHAPTER ONE

The ring of her phone cut through the night. The air buzzed with the sound of traffic and the pulse of the music from the party below. Yet still, her phone sounded louder than it should, too loud. She rummaged through her skintight, black spandex suit until she retrieved it. Worried it might be Simon, she answered without checking the screen.

"Hello?" she hissed.

"L? Is that you?"

For a second, a paralyzingly long second, she thought it was Christy-Anne. The voice didn't sound like her and the person on the phone didn't tell her to go fuck herself immediately, but the woman had a terrible habit of calling at the worst possible times. Like when she was standing on the rooftop of a hotel, acting as accomplice and lookout for a heist.

But it wasn't Christy-Anne. Lucille didn't work with the pop star anymore and considering she'd changed her phone number since her return to the celebrity spin doctor business, a call from her would be unwelcome.

"This is Lucille. Who's this?" she asked, glancing over her shoulder at the roof access door. The likelihood of anyone inside the hotel hearing her phone conversation was low, but she could hope. After an eternity of waiting alone in the dark, she'd give anything for something to happen, even if it was the job going south. Or especially if it was the job going south?

"It's Jasmine," said the caller.

"Jasmine?" Of all the clients to call her late at night, she wouldn't expect it to be her.

Jasmine Lawson was a big deal in Hollywood. Her first role was starring in the period piece *Revolt at Sundown* where she'd played a prostitute who ended up leading a textile worker's revolution. The film was studded with established stars and had earned a record-setting number of award nominations. Jasmine herself swept the Best Actress category for the entire season. As did the director, Michel Polce.

Lucille became involved when Jasmine decided to finish high school at the private academy near her hometown, away from the spotlight and the media. On Michel's advice, Jasmine had sought Lucille's help in keeping her whereabouts quiet until she graduated. Any paparazzo who tried to get the scoop on her found themselves at the mercy of her spin doctor.

After two photographers and a celebrity gossip blog had their credibility eviscerated, no one else had made any attempts to find the young actress.

"Yeah..." Jasmine's voice was hesitant.

"Who found you?" said Lucille, clenching her fist reflexively.

There was a pause.

"Was it *Teen Watch*? I knew they wouldn't stay away. I will gut those motherfuckers. Professionally speaking."

"No, no one found me."

Lucille started to stalk along the building edge, her knee-high boots silent against the concrete. "Start from the beginning," she said in the most encouraging voice she could manage.

Jasmine took a deep breath. "Well... Okay. Here's what happened. So, I've been having issues with some of the football players here. It's a private school football team, so they're not great, but they still act like complete assholes most of the time."

"Sure," said Lucille, trying to connect with her client by thinking back to her own high school days.

She'd dated a football player, but that didn't seem like a useful thing to add to the conversation.

"Earlier tonight, maybe three hours ago? I decided enough is enough. I'm sick to death of them getting away with making sexist comments and sharing unsolicited dick pics and just acting like they own the place. So, I borrowed my parents' Porsche even though I technically still don't have a driver's license."

Jasmine paused again, seemingly waiting for Lucille's reaction to this announcement.

"Is that it? Because if it is, that's easy. Barely even a blip of an issue." Lucille glanced toward the access door, but all remained still and empty.

"Yeah, no. There's more."

Lucille waited. On the street below, a car blared its horn.

"I drove to the school, wrote *fuck you sexist assholes* in lighter fluid on the football field, and lit in on fire."

Lucille stopped. She blinked a few times. This wasn't the first time one of her clients had called about something they'd lit on fire. Usually, it was her boy band clients and they'd been trying to create a cool effect for a music video, but things had gone horribly wrong. Or they drunkenly burned their clothes and were stranded naked at a loft party in Brooklyn. It'd happened more than once and, therefore, way too many times.

This situation was a first for her, but in a positive way.

"Cool," she said, and meant it.

Jasmine laughed, but it was a brief, high-pitched laugh that betrayed her nerves. "Yeah, it does look pretty cool."

Lucille frowned. "Are you still there right now?"

"Yes."

"Jasmine, you are a wonderfully talented person, and I'm all about this act of righteous vandalism, but you need to get out of there. Now."

"I know, I know. But here's the thing. I was about to leave when I noticed a security camera pointed like right on the field. I definitely got caught on tape, and I'm pretty positive they'll know it's me." Her words poured out in an anxious stream as she got to the point of her story.

Ah. That was why Jasmine called her. Not to confess to borrowing the car or lighting up the football field, but because—if she was caught on camera—the school would probably expel her. If the footage was leaked, there was a good chance the general public would be on her side, but those who weren't could get nasty. If the footage wasn't leaked and all the media reported was her expulsion, things would get even uglier. There was only one possible solution.

"So, I called you," Jasmine was saying, "I thought you might be awake since you keep really odd hours, and... do you think I should break into the school and wipe the footage?"

That was not the possible solution.

"Uh, no. Don't do that. Take it from someone who knows, breaking into places gets you into a whole big mess unless you know exactly what you're do-ing and have an airtight exit strategy," said Lucille. She'd resumed her pacing, speeding up as the idea coalesced in her mind. "Here's what you're going to do. First, leave the school right now."

"Are you sure?"

"Jasmine, I'm always sure. Are you driving away?"

Lucille heard the soft purr of a luxury vehicle engine.

"Yes."

"Good. Now, tomorrow, if, and only if, you get called into the headmaster's office and accused of vandalizing the field, I want you to deny absolutely everything. Even if they have hard evidence to ID you, you still deny ever being there. Most likely, given the reputation of the school, they won't want to get law enforcement involved and will instead try to quietly expel you. If that happens, you threaten to mobilize your fan base against the school unless they drop the whole incident and things change."

"Oh, like holding these assholes accountable for their sexist behavior?" For the first time in their conversation, Jasmine's tone was something other than hesitant.

"Exactly."

"Nice. What do you mean by mobilizing my fans?"

Lucille grinned. She loved this part of her job. "Leave all of that to me. I'll send you everything you need tonight. What to tell the headmaster, what to say to your publicist or parents or whoever gets involved, and a couple of different messages to send out to your fans through your socials if we have to go that route."

Jasmine was silent.

Lucille wondered if she'd lost her. She even checked her phone to make sure the call was still connected.

"What if it doesn't work and it all gets out?"

"First of all, it's going to work. I don't do things that don't work. Second, you just lit the fucking football field on fire. I think you'll be fine." It may very well be the most inspiring speech Lucille had ever given. Usually, she was talking someone down or scrambling to come up with a feasible solution for the shitstorm they'd started. It wasn't often she got to empower her clients to make an actual change, and she found it wasn't bad.

As soon as she ended the call, she had her notes file open and was drafting at lightning speed. She was so engaged in her task, she didn't hear the door open and close as someone joined her on the roof.

"Have you been on the phone this entire time?" said a voice behind her.

Chapter Two

E*arlier*

"Noah thinks we need to go right to the source. We're going to steal the flash drive, and we need you," Simon said, his normally calm expression lit with excitement.

"That's the dumbest idea I've ever heard."

Even though it was mediated through the computer screen, Lucille could feel her uncle's responding glare. "Lucy, we agreed to try things Noah's way for a while. He may be onto something, and I, for one, want to see how it goes."

"If you want to run around breaking into hotel rooms, be my guest. I have more important things to do. Like my job." In Lucille's mind, their compromise was that Simon and Noah were going to try things Noah's way and she was going to go about her own business, running the LA branch of their business the right way.

"Noah says you're a crucial part of the plan."

"Noah can suck it." Not her greatest comeback, but then Noah brought out the worst in her.

"Lucille," Simon began with a dramatic sigh, "you know I hate doing this, darling, but, well, we need you."

"What are you saying?"

Simon took a deep breath. "If you don't help us, I will be forced to tell everyone what happened at the Save the Lemurs charity event."

"You wouldn't dare." She never should've told Simon about it in the first place. Simon Anton Rule of Spin Doctoring Number 27: Never tell anyone secrets they can use against you. Especially family members.

The next thing she knew, Lucille was flying to the Bay area with her black spandex bodysuit and a suitcase full of instant regret. She was beginning to suspect her relationship with her uncle was dysfunctional.

A business rival was blackmailing one of Simon and Noah's clients. This rival had incriminating photos of the client on a flash drive and was threatening to leak the photos unless the client helped with the forceful takeover of a third company.

Lucille, if it had been her client, would, first of all, not have taken the case. The whole thing seemed to be about men being assholes and throwing around their money and power. Boring. If she had taken the case, she would allow the photos to be leaked, then spin them back onto the rival, making that guy look bad and take the fall for the whole thing.

Noah's plan, however, was to break into the rival's hotel room and steal the flash drive while the man was attending an important late-night after-party in the ballroom on the first floor. Which was how Lucille ended up lurking on a dimly lit roof, being scolded by Noah Harkin.

"Seriously, have you been on the phone the whole time I was gone?" Noah, a Korean American former private investigator, scowled at her. He wore his black hair in a spiky swoop, his brown eyes dark and glaring, his jaw clenched, arms crossed. Tonight, he wore all black—black jeggings, a tight-fitting black shirt, and a black jacket over it. The look accentuated his hotness in a way Lucille found utterly unnecessary.

She crossed her arms too. "Not that it's any concern of yours, but I had some important business to take care of."

He stalked toward her, his scowl intensifying. She hated that he was taller than her, even in her stiletto boots.

"It is my concern when you were supposed to be on lookout," Noah accused in a loud whisper. They were, after all, still at the scene of the crime. If a crime had been committed at all. He seemed more interested in fighting with her than letting her know if he'd been successful in stealing the drive.

"Well then, excuse me, but if I wasn't on lookout, what the fuck do you think I'm doing up here on this roof?"

"You were supposed to be in the hallway outside the room I broke into."

Lucille had two options. The first was to admit she hadn't been paying attention when he'd laid out the details and apologize. The second was to deny the whole thing and get inordinately pissed at him. She rarely admitted her mistakes and certainly wasn't about to admit anything to him. "And how exactly was I supposed to know that?"

"It's the logical place for you to be. Why would you be on the roof when I'm breaking into a room inside the hotel?"

Lucille sighed. She didn't like this conversation and was done with it. True, being on lookout inside the hotel did make more sense. Or it would to someone who was actually invested in this case, which she wasn't, and she didn't know how to communicate that more clearly to her so-called coworkers. She could tell him she hadn't intentionally ignored his plan. Or not. "You seem to be suffering under the assumption that anything about this is logical. I assume you got the drive, and no one saw you?"

Noah nodded, still glaring.

"Then let's get out of here before we actually do get caught," she said and set about abseiling down the back of the building to the deserted alley below.

When they reached the street, Noah retrieved the backpack he'd stashed earlier and stowed the climbing gear. Lucille led the way to what was supposed to be their rendezvous spot with Simon. Only the street where he was meant to be waiting with the surveillance SUV was completely Simon-free.

"What the fuck?" Noah stopped in the shadowed entrance of a closed office building, scanning the parked cars.

Lucille momentarily felt bad for Noah. He, unaccustomed as he was to working with the Antons, was having a rough night. "Maybe he didn't know the plan either."

"He knew the plan. It seems that he, like you, decided to go off script," Noah said with a growl.

Lucille shrugged even though he wasn't looking at her. "Probably. It's what we do about eighty percent of the time. If that doesn't work with your anal need to control everything, you're welcome to quit at any time." She was stretching the truth. Not about Simon, per se. It was accurate that he never did anything according to plan. But she did, and she liked plans and control possibly more than Noah did. She didn't like him being in control of the plan, though.

"I see how it is," he said, looking at her.

"How what is?"

"You're furious Simon asked me to join the team. You want me to get fed up and quit." He moved toward her as he spoke. It was dark in the doorway, but he came close enough that she could see his face illuminated by the streetlights. His expression was one of intensity and frustration, and dammit, he made it look so attractive. Noah was muscular, that she already knew, and the outfit he wore put those muscles on display in a way that didn't disappoint. He was clean-shaven, and his brown skin looked smooth and soft. It was soft, Lucille knew that already. It was something she was trying to forget.

"How'd you guess?" she asked sarcastically, trying not to remember the way his mouth felt on hers. Those were things she wasn't thinking about. Ever.

"Oh, I don't know, maybe because you bring it up every time you talk to Simon? Maybe because you've been avoiding me?"

"It's been a month since we rescued Michel. We don't even live in the same city. That hardly counts as avoiding." Why was she defending herself to him? What did she care what he thought or that he noticed she wasn't speaking to him?

"I know you don't want me working with you and Simon," Noah said as he moved closer, casting his face back into shadow.

Lucille kept her icy expression and tone that she was perfecting during her interactions with him. "Well, you're right about that. But then statistically everyone is right about something once."

Noah laughed, and it was a hollow, false sound. "You're hilarious, you know that?"

"What the fuck are you talking about?" Lucille could play games all day long, but she didn't want to play with him. She wanted to find Simon and get the hell out of there.

"You. Pretending this has nothing to do with what happened between us. With the electricity that's still there," Noah said, his eyes intense.

Was it a rule that everything that came out of some people's mouths, no matter how lame, insulting, or just plain stupid it was, sounded sexy? Lucille wondered if she should get her head checked for a potential concussion. She must have hit it at some point while climbing around on the roof of the hotel and now was suffering from a delayed reaction to the cranial trauma. It was the only explanation for that kind of thinking where Noah Harkin was involved. "Oh, please. Does that line actually work?"

Noah shrugged. "Sometimes. I mean, not usually, when it's just a line. But I'm serious here. There's something between us. And I, for one, don't run from a challenge."

"And I do?" Lucille asked. She was worked up. Worked up as in she wanted to jump Noah's bones in the street or worked up in that she wanted to punch him in the face and run away? A lot of both.

"Nah, you'd rather sit back and make up stories to help people avoid challenges."

"That's literally what our job is."

"Was. That's what our job was," Noah said, his voice taking on a new energy, "I'm trying to offer something new, an upgraded service package, if you will."

"You sound like you're pimping yourself out," Lucille said. On one hand, Noah's ideas for the business weren't bad. They were risky, dangerous, and threatened the future of their operation, but they weren't bad. If it was a year ago and Lucille didn't have friends or family, she'd probably go for Noah's schemes. It wasn't a year ago though, and she had things to lose. "As long as you stay away from my clients," she said, infusing her voice with quiet authority.

"Anton. We're supposed to be a team on this. We're trying to keep rich people from destroying their careers, and I'm merely offering a more effective and lucrative way of doing that."

"How many times do I have to tell you not to call me Anton?" she said, her entire body taut with the tension of holding back. She still didn't know whether she was going to punch him or kiss him, but both were equally likely to hurt.

"Lucille." The word rolled off his tongue like it was something he was tasting, savoring. Her name. He was tasting and savoring her name. It was heady, and her pulse sped up.

They were inches apart, and she could hear his breath, quick and shallow, like he couldn't catch it, couldn't recover as he looked at her.

Lucille knew she either had to step backward and avoid the contact or do this her way. Whatever Noah may taunt her with, she wasn't one to shy from a challenge, and he was issuing exactly that. In a swift move, she pushed against his chest, walking them backward until he was pressed against the stone wall of the building. She was strong, but so was he, and she suspected he was letting her push him, letting her have her way with him. That too was heady and reminded her of that night...

Not breaking eye contact, she closed the remaining distance between them and kissed him. Her eyes closed, and she felt his mouth beneath hers, giving back all the force and desire she put into the kiss. As she gripped the sides of his jacket, she'd heard his hands slap against the wall but now felt one of them trail up the side of her body, lightly, too lightly. It was tender in a way she didn't want him to be.

She pushed off him, breaking the contact and retreating. He leaned against the building and let out a long, audible breath.

The kiss ended not a moment too soon. A black SUV pulled up a few feet from where they stood.

The tinted front window rolled down to reveal Simon, his silvery blond hair swept to one side, his eyebrows raised, and his expression one of bemusement.

When Lucille first saw the vehicle they'd be using that night, she'd been surprised and impressed. In the past few months when they'd been forced into various rescue and recon missions, Simon had seemed to favor the shitty, rented white van look. Lucille had asked him about the upgrade, and he'd confessed it had been JP's doing. JP, like Lucille, didn't understand why their job had to include so much running around and spying, but had said, if Simon was going to insist on doing that shit, he at least needed to not look like that was what he was doing. Thus, the shiny new SUV.

Of course, JP wasn't going to let Simon use all the high-tech equipment his company, LT Tech, made without some idea of what Simon was using it for. And since Simon wasn't any more used to being held accountable than Lucille was, he hadn't told JP about their little evening outing. Which meant, on the occasions when Simon chose to ignore both his phone and the rendezvous instructions, they were forced to wait and see if he'd show.

"Simon, where have you been?" Lucille hissed, her voice more indignant than she'd have liked. She didn't look at Noah and wasn't going to.

"What do you mean where have I been? Where have you been?" Simon retorted. It was a classic Anton reaction—respond to accusations with more accusations.

There was a sigh off to her right, but she didn't look over. "According to the plan, you were supposed to be waiting for us on this street," Noah said. His voice didn't sound at all affected by what they'd been doing.

"That is, relatively speaking what I was doing," Simon said with a serious nod.

Lucille knew better than to say anything. She hoped Noah did, too.

After a long pause in which she sensed Noah was struggling to come up with a response to Simon's nonsense, she said, "Instead of standing around here, let's just go. You can argue about the details in the debriefing."

"Which I will be leading," Noah grumbled as he followed her into the SUV and Simon careened down the road, tires squealing.

Chapter Three

*L*ate *is better than never*, thought Brett as he looked out over the Pacific. *And I really do need a vacation.*

The last time he'd been at a private island resort, the one he was now banned from, vacationing had been a distant mirage on the horizon. After all, he'd been injured, slightly delirious, and spent most of the short stay avoiding explosions and searching for his horrid cousin. What a difference a few months had made.

Soon, the island would come into view. A tiny island off the coast of Hawaii, home to one of the top-rated resorts in the world and their destination for this long weekend.

Turning from the window, Brett found Michel watching him from the facing seat. Michel Polce was dressed in a pale-pink linen suit that looked soft, comfortable, and utterly sinful. His white shirt was open at the top and his perfectly sculpted features held an expression of calm amusement.

"What?" Brett asked, shifting in his seat. There were times when he looked at Michel and couldn't imagine what Michel saw in him. Partially, this feeling came from his general self-deprecating nature. Then there was the fact that Michel was gorgeous, insanely talented, wealthy beyond imagine, and a delight to be around, while Brett was a scruffy scientist whose clothes were always wrinkled and who generally put his foot in his mouth during social interactions. It shouldn't work for a romantic relationship, and yet, here they were, finally making good on their proclamation of running away together.

"I'm remembering the last time we were headed to a private island," said Michel, "how different things were then."

Brett snorted. "No kidding. Shit, I still thought I was completely straight."

"Thankfully, you came to your senses on that." Michel grinned at him.

Brett's heart threatened to beat out of his chest and his whole body lit up. Michel's smiles were potent, a fact well documented by many a magazine feature.

They were taking things slow.

When the initial plan to run off immediately after the not-sex-party crime club meeting ended in Michel getting held at gunpoint by the club president, they'd decided to take things down a few dozen notches, to gently navigate their way from friendship into romance.

With Michel smiling at him like that, though, looking like sex in an airplane seat, Brett had no idea whose terrible idea it was to apply the brakes. After all, there was no one else on Michel's private jet. They could have been fooling around this entire time. Instead, Brett sat in his seat and Michel in his, and there was no funny business whatsoever. The rush of anxiety and the constant internal whisper he wasn't enough reminded him it was his idea to go slow. Because he was terrified.

Earlier in the flight, Michel had been frowning at his phone, the little lines between his eyes showing his concentration and concern. On Brett, those frown lines were becoming permanent wrinkles, signs he was getting older. On Michel, they didn't last, his brown skin returning to a smooth canvas where things like wrinkles and laugh lines wouldn't dare to tread. Brett had laugh lines. He found gray hairs each morning and wondered why the hell those were turning up so soon in his life.

Michel didn't. His hair was black and styled at all times—right now it was shaved on the sides and longer on top. His features were angular without being bony, his lips full and pale pink. He had a single ear piercing, but he didn't look like a pirate or a hipster, he looked moody, creative, and aloof. His body, carefully maintained through exercise and the strict diet Brett was still adjusting to, seemed to be sculpted out of marble. Brett had seen him a few times without a shirt and his muscles were present, but not prominent. His abs were well defined without being rock hard, and he had body hair but was by no means hairy. And his ass... well, that was a work of art.

"Brett," Michel had said, looking up from his phone. "You're staring at me again."

He didn't say it in a mean way, merely an affectionate admonishment.

Brett's face reddened. "Right. Sorry."

Michel shook his head. "There's no need to be sorry. I don't mind you staring at me. But I do need to get this done before we arrive so I can give you my full attention."

The thing no one wanted to know about Michel was that he worked hard. He made every public appearance seem effortless, but the truth was, his persona required constant upkeep. Since they'd known each other, Michel had always done his research before going into any situation. He showed up at a meeting knowing as much as he could about the other attendees. He dedicated himself to each part, agonized over every word he wrote, and took his directing very seriously.

Brett's theory, although Michel had never said so, was that some of that serious, all-consuming concentration on his work was why Sylvia had snapped and tried to kill him. He didn't know his cousin well, but he could guess she'd grown bored with Michel, wanting the extravagant lifestyle but not the sacrifices that came with it. So, she'd tried, and failed, to get rid of Michel and keep the money.

Brett didn't mind that Michel worked a lot nor resented his concentration. He himself worked long hours and got absorbed in his projects without thinking about meals or the people in his life. It did, however, make for a challenge when they were trying to get a new relationship off the ground. Hopefully, being alone for a weekend on a gorgeous resort island would change that.

A *new relationship*. The lump of anxiety threatened to choke him. He wondered how long it would take Michel to realize he wasn't worth the trouble. He had it on good authority, namely Lucille had yelled it at him during five of their seven break-ups, he wasn't a great boyfriend. Yet, they'd gotten through all of that and were still friends, so maybe he wasn't a complete lost cause? No, he wasn't going to play the comparison game. *Stay in the here and now*, he reminded himself.

"Brett," Michel said, drawing his name out in a warning.

He'd been staring again. Brett broke his gaze and turned his focus to the text he'd gotten before they boarded the plane. He'd gotten a number of texts, mostly from Lucille and all in the vein of her wanting to murder Noah and/or Simon. Possibly both of them. Knowing his friend and ex as well as he did, this outpouring of emotion toward Noah meant the guy had gotten under her skin. It would all end in sex or death. He hoped it was the former.

But Lucille's texts weren't what perplexed him. It was a single line from an unknown number, generic enough to be a mistake but specific enough to be intentional—*Let me know when you arrive at the resort, Brett.*

He put his phone away without responding. It was a wrong number, a message meant for another Brett going to a different resort. It had to be.

The plane landed at an airport comprised of a tiny building and a grassy landing strip. After they disembarked, the pilot taxied the plane over to the parking area, which Brett thought was a joke. It was not. A row of small jets and helicopters were neatly stowed behind the small building, waiting to cater to their owner's every whim.

"Does everyone own a private plane?" he muttered.

A private car took them to the resort, a huge building of white sandstone called "The Reef." The front entrance was framed by imposing columns, the interior a dazzling array of white marble and bright, tropical flowers. Personally, Brett found it too gaudy for his taste, but then he'd never be able to afford the place on his own, so who was he to judge?

He started toward the front desk. Michel caught his arm.

"Where are you going?"

"To check in."

Michel shook his head and gestured at a man in the suit waiting some feet to their left. "He'll take us to our room."

Brett knew he shouldn't be surprised any longer, but he was. "So, you don't even check in at hotels anymore?"

Michel laughed and smiled at him. "No."

Brett knew there was little to no chance he was ever going to get used to being in Michel's world. As they followed the man through the glass hallway connecting the main area of the hotel to what Brett assumed were the outrageously expensive suites, his panic started to rise again. What was he doing there? Yes, he'd been friends with Michel for a long time, but he'd never let Michel pay for him. He was used to feeling inadequate next to Michel, but never quite this inadequate.

Before Brett could think himself into a full-blown attack, they arrived at their suite. It was at the end of the corridor, on the second floor. The man unlocked the door, handed them the keys, and disappeared as quietly as he'd arrived. Brett took a deep breath and followed Michel into the room.

The suite was enormous. The first room housed a sitting area decorated in deep teal with gold brocade furniture and a glass-topped coffee table. To the right was another room, the bedroom, which Brett chose to ignore for the present. The sitting room opened out onto a large balcony overlooking the ocean. Brett took in all of this and then returned to the issue of the color scheme.

"Michel..." he began. "We aren't by any chance, in the Mermaid suite, are we?"

A bellhop who'd followed them from the car and was unloading their bags into the entryway answered his question. "Yes, you are, sir. It's one of the finest suites in the hotel."

"Oh," said Brett, pausing until the bellhop left. When the door was closed again, he added, "It's a lot."

"What, this?" Michel waved a hand around at the teal and gold. "Nonsense, Brett. Seems totally normal to me."

Brett was all prepared to embark into further self-deprecation when he caught Michel's smirk and realized he was joking. Brett rolled his eyes and chuckled. The tension threatening to draw him under released. At least until Brett caught a new expression in Michel's eyes. Michel's gaze was heated, powerfully intent on him, and the tension was back in a different flavor.

Brett swallowed. "We're on vacation. Just the two of us."

"Yes, we are," Michel replied, and then he too swallowed.

Brett didn't know who moved first, but they reached for each other and it didn't matter who initiated the kiss because then they were kissing and it was glorious. Michel was a few inches taller and Brett leaned his head back into Michel's kiss. His mouth was hot, soft, and tasted like chocolate. One of his hands was in Brett's hair and the other was on his back, holding him close. Brett rested his hands on Michel's hips and he tugged at him as he licked into his mouth. Michel let out a little gasp of a moan, and Brett shivered. His fingers gripped Michel, wanting to pull him even closer, even though they were already plastered together. He toyed with the edge of Michel's linen suit and then swept his hand under the jacket and tugged at the pink shirt.

Then Michel wasn't messing around and his hands were under Brett's t-shirt, scorching his bare skin.

Brett broke away for a second. "Hey, no fair. You're wearing more clothes than I am."

Michel, his mouth red and swollen from kisses, his gaze a little unfocused, said, "There's a solution for that, you know."

"Oh, really? Do tell."

"Nudity, Brett. You, me, naked," said Michel, and he wasn't kidding.

Brett tried to push down the trepidation that accompanied his arousal. He didn't doubt his attraction to Michel, nor Michel's attraction to him. But he was nervous. This was his best friend and also, yeah, he was a little nervous about having sex with the man for the first time. "That does seem like an apt solution," he managed to reply.

Michel's thumb traced Brett's mouth, and he stopped talking. And breathing for a bit. "You know, last time we were on an island together, we didn't take full advantage of the amenities. The beds, for example."

Brett laughed, and it came out weak. "We were a tad preoccupied."

Michel sighed and stepped back.

Brett reached for him. He didn't want Michel to react like that, hadn't at all intended to ruin the mood with reminders of his past. And yet, had he?

"Yes, and I was foolishly chasing someone who was trying to kill me."

Oh Lord, thought Brett. *Michel's getting into one of his melancholy moods.* What about the sexy times that, five seconds ago, seemed so imminent?

He didn't have a chance to protest. There was a knock on the door. Brett looked at it, startled. "I'll get it," he said out of habit.

Michel frowned. "Okay." He picked up a couple of suitcases and went into the bedroom.

Brett was in the process of berating himself for being a dumbass, and an idiot, and whatever other names he could think of when he opened the door. And stared. If it were an actual ghost, he couldn't have been more shocked and horrified. After all, it'd been years since they'd seen each other, two years to be precise. And that occasion hadn't exactly ended in sunshine and rainbows.

"Hey, Brett," said his sister Patience.

CHAPTER FOUR

Two months earlier

The first time Lucille met Noah, they'd both been attending a charity gala for an animal. It was a type of lemur that, up until this event, Lucille had neither heard of nor cared about. Her clients, however, cared a lot about this lemur. So much so they were working on an entire island sanctuary for the creature. They'd requested a couple of the lemurs be flown in for the event, despite the protests of the conservationists who said that flying lemurs most of the way around the world was maybe the worst thing that could be done for the animals.

Personally, Lucille agreed with the conservationists. In the six months since she had been held at gunpoint by Sylvia Stanton and shot by her detective ex-boyfriend, she'd melted a tiny bit. Not enough to ever be accused of being friendly, but she didn't hold the entire world in contempt quite as much. At least not the lemurs. So, she persuaded her clients to settle for some lemurs who were already in a nearby zoo and hoped that would be the last she heard about them. It wasn't, of course. Lemurs dominated the conversation so much that, by the time the gala came around, Lucille had run through her backup reserves of patience and was wondering why she'd ever left spin doctoring.

As usual, it took Lucille a minute to remember she didn't need to be incognito at events. The instinct to disappear when anyone approached her was still there, waiting in case she needed to act on it. But as a publicist, a highly paid publicist with a burgeoning career and a skyrocketing trajectory, she was meant to be seen. This wasn't a film premiere, an award show, or an exclusive house party at a mansion in Beverly Hills. This was a charity event with executives, politicians, and anyone else looking to be seen. She'd spent most of the week refereeing the argument between her clients and the lemur rescuers. Hell, she was wearing a black, sequined pantsuit that stood out even in the crowded finery.

She drained her glass of champagne.

When she was a spin doctor, she never drank during the events. There were too many opportunities for slip-ups. But once she'd seen the dull, mundane underbelly of going straight and working for a PR company, she drank at events. It helped her forget that, in an unusual turn of events for Lucille Anton, her life was pretty crappy at the moment.

She'd broken up with Brett again that morning. He wasn't moving out. She wasn't moving out. They didn't know anyone else in the city besides coworkers who they wouldn't even consider hanging out with outside of the office. Which left only each other.

She sighed. They never should have started dating. She cared about Brett, she really did, but if she dated him for one more day, she was going to blow shit up.

The ballroom glittered, one lemur chewed on some leaves, another posed for pictures and then tried to steal purses, and the baby lemur fell head-over-heels to a chorus of sympathetic *awws*. Checks were flying and the host was beaming.

Lucille grabbed another glass from a passing tray. Before, she never would have accepted a drink off a passed tray. Her drinks used to be so fresh the ice hadn't even dared to start melting or she wouldn't drink it. How far the mighty had fallen.

Her coworker moved through the crowd toward her. She didn't want to talk to him. He liked to tell people that he was only a PR agent until his app took off. He had to be constantly reminded not to pitch to their clients. Lucille abhorred him fiercely.

She turned to dissolve into the crowd, but the third glass of champagne was catching up to her. Instead of slipping gracefully away, she careened into someone.

"Whoa," the someone said, stepping backward and putting out a hand to steady her.

Lucille looked at the person. A man, Asian, with swooped black hair, a designer tux, and a concerned expression. "I'm so sorry," she said in her most bubbly voice, planning to charm and escape.

"No harm done," said the man, his face splitting into a self-assured grin.

Lucille's heart jumped, her breath caught, and she could have sworn the rest of the room vanished. It lasted only a second and was probably the result of the champagne. She didn't know what to say and so she did something she never did, she walked away. Not a moment too soon. She could almost feel her coworker's breath on the back of her neck as she slipped out of the room.

The second time she saw the guy was after she'd returned to the ballroom to listen to her client's speech. He stood by the bar, alone, scanning the room with a lazy casualness that put her on edge immediately. He was looking for something. Their eyes met and, although she'd never admit it in court, she felt a little flutter of excitement. This mysterious, gorgeous guy was up to something, and she was going to find out what it was.

Her client began to speak. He rambled, he pontificated. Lucille listened enough to note if he strayed off into any of the topics he had been told, in no uncertain terms, not to bring up. Otherwise, she didn't give a fuck what the man said.

In her peripheral vision, she saw the guy leave the bar. He strolled across the ballroom heading either to the bathroom or out for some fresh air. Lucille wasn't fooled. She followed him, keeping to the edge of the room, one eye trained on the stage in the event her client noticed her departure. Rising star or not, the firm cared about things like her leaving early, and she hated that oversight most of all.

Out in the opulent lobby, she scanned for the guy. She almost missed him ducking into a room down a hallway to her right. She followed, noting the hall housed conference rooms, and the door the man had disappeared behind was another of the same. As her hand reached toward the handle, she paused. What the hell was she doing? She was following a complete stranger at a gala and was it really because she thought he was up to something or because she thought he was attractive? Odds were he'd gone into the room to make a phone call in private.

Lucille was about to turn and go back to the ballroom and remind herself she was in San Francisco, not Hollywood, when she heard voices through the door. More specifically, she heard a voice she knew. Someone she hadn't seen at the event and who, to her knowledge, had no reason to be in this city at all.

It was the voice of a onetime client, a musician with, as she recalled, a rather nasty drug problem. She paused. She hadn't heard from the musician client in years. He was one of those classic rock guys who thought the drugs helped his music. He hadn't liked her method of doing things, and frankly, she hadn't liked him one bit. Last she'd heard of him, he was trying to start up a new band and claimed to be releasing an album within the next year. And now he was at this event, shut in a private room with the man she'd been following.

If it had been another client, Lucille would have marched into the room and demanded to know what was going on. For this one, she decided to sit back and see what happened next. She chose a chair out in the lobby with a clear view of the conference room door. A magazine sat on the table next to her. She flipped through it idly, watching and waiting. Should her PR coworker find her now, she'd have no explanation of what she was doing and why. The lack of an explanation had never stopped her before, and it wouldn't now. It was time to dust off her spin doctor skills. To leave the conventional PR roles to those who wanted them and get back to what mattered. Scandal.

Twenty minutes passed. The door of the conference room opened and her former client appeared, his face stormy, his progress guided by the firm grip of her mystery man. They headed away from the lobby and out an exit at the far end of the hall.

It took all of Lucille's carefully perfected control not to sneak after them and try to overhear what had happened. She glanced around the lobby as she flipped the pages of her magazine. The front desk staff were staring at their computers, answering phone calls, and generally noticing nothing. Diagonally from where she sat was the hotel restaurant where voices and laughter drifted through the beige modernism. A woman sat in a chair against the wall, talking on her cell. No one had noticed.

The exit door opened again, and the mystery man returned, alone. He walked down the hallway toward the lobby and the ballroom beyond, not a hair out of place, his expression one of cool indifference.

He didn't seem to notice Lucille sitting on the white leather couch. As he drew near, she said, in her most bubbly voice, "What was *that* all about?"

The guy looked at her, startled. She looked back at him, waiting.

"What was what all about?" he asked slowly. His voice was deep and hesitant.

Lucille sat back and set her magazine aside pointedly. Her suit glittered under the fluorescents. "Are you a detective? FBI? CIA? Mercenary? Bounty hunter?"

The man's thin mouth was set, his brown eyes cold. He sat down on the couch across from her and leaned forward. When he spoke, it was in a hiss, "I don't know what you're talking about."

Lucille smiled. "Of course, you do. The rest of the people at this hotel might not have seen you and the lead singer of Cranium just now, but I make it a point to notice these things."

He frowned and leaned back a bit, clearly caught off guard by something she'd said. "How does a corporate PR agent know the lead singer of Cranium?"

Lucille wasn't surprised he knew who she was. If he knew more about her than her work in corporate PR, he held it back. Odds were, he didn't. After all, there were only a select few who knew Lucille Anton, Celebrity Spin Doctor, and they were bound by ironclad contracts not to talk. But, since he wasn't going to answer her questions, she wasn't going to answer his. Petty but then, what did she have to lose in this conversation? It was all for her own entertainment. "You've heard of me."

"All of Northern California has heard of you, Ms. Anton," the guy responded with heavy sarcasm.

Lucille smirked. "Clever. So, since you have the advantage, why don't you tell me who you are?"

He opened his mouth, but she cut him off.

"And not the fake identity you're using. The truth."

He closed his mouth, pursed his lips, and finally said, "Noah Harkin, private investigator. How did you know I'm using a fake identity?"

Lucille debated telling him where his slip-up was. If he was really there to meet the musician, he would have left after he'd delivered his dirt, job done. Since he'd returned, it indicated he was there on other business and the musician encounter had been a lucky coincidence. The confrontation had been done so unobtrusively it wasn't hard to guess he was trying not to blow his cover. Instead, she raised an eyebrow and continued her interrogation. "So, what are you really here about? Investigating someone?"

Noah frowned and leaned back against his couch, mirroring her position. "That's my business. And even if it weren't private, why the hell would I tell you? You basically work for the media."

Lucille gave him a withering glare. He was starting to piss her off. "I do not work for the media. I work with the media. There's a difference."

"Not for me."

A thought struck her unpleasantly. "You're not here for the lemurs, are you?"

He looked at her like she was nuts. "Isn't this whole event for the lemurs?"

So no then. She didn't bother explaining she wasn't talking about lemurs in general but about the specific lemurs at the event. "Never mind. Are you investigating my clients?"

She dared him to ask who her clients were. To pretend he didn't know as much about her as he could gather.

This conversation highlighted the other unpleasant side effect of working for a legit PR company. This PI knew things about her. There were records of who she worked with and what she did. If someone went digging too deep, they'd eventually find everything. She couldn't let Noah get too interested in her. At least not professionally.

"Not exactly, no."

Interesting. "Great, well, in that case, I think we're all set here." She stood up and made to leave.

Noah grasped her arm.

Lucille looked down at his hand and then slowly back at him, showing him exactly how much she did not like this move.

He released her. "Wait just a moment. You haven't told me how you know the lead singer of Cranium or why you were out here spying on me."

Lucille laughed. "Oh, please. Don't flatter yourself. I wasn't spying on you."

Noah's jaw tightened.

"As for Cranium, let's just say I'm a fan." It was a dumb lie. The thought of anyone, even an independent detective, looking into her was taking hold in her mind and causing her to make silly mistakes.

"No, you're not," Noah said firmly. "No one is a fan of Cranium."

Lucille smirked to show she was messing with him.

Noah stood and turned to walk back toward the conference rooms. He looked at her over his shoulder. "Are you coming?"

Lucille considered telling him he could fuck off. But then it was her own fault, her own damn boredom that had led to this interaction in the first place and, if she didn't see it through, who knew what questions he'd start asking. If she had just let Noah go back to the ballroom and carry on with his investigation, he would go on believing she was a PR agent and nothing else.

So, she followed him down the hall. They stopped in the doorway of one of the rooms, and he turned around to look at her.

Despite her heels, he was still taller than her, and she hated that.

"Are you trying to play me or something?" he asked. "Do you think I'm that gullible?"

Yes. Out loud, she sighed heavily. "What do you want from me, Mr. Harkin?"

"I want to know how you know a notorious drug dealer," Noah said, his voice calm with an undercurrent of annoyance. "And I think you should answer honestly, Ms. Anton."

Ah, so the musician had turned to dealing the drugs. Well, that cleared one thing up at least. "Why should I tell you? I don't owe you anything."

He looked her slowly up and down, his dark gaze dragging over her with a clear, deliberate attempt at unnerving her. "I'm a PI, Ms. Anton. Don't you think I can recognize when someone's hiding something?"

It was the sexiest thing that had happened to her in months. "He was once a client of mine. A long time ago. Pre-drug dealing."

Noah didn't look convinced. "Up until six months ago, no one had heard of you."

Lucille laughed. "Up until six months ago, I wasn't anyone in the business. You can read all about it if you want to. My big break, my meteoric rise to the top of PR, the whole inspirational story. It's amazing how people pay no attention to you until you land LT Tech as a client."

Noah continued to frown at her.

Lucille found she cared more than she should, more than she thought she would, about Noah believing her. She considered telling him some truth. Not all of it, not even most of it, but a little bit. Just enough to get him off her trail.

"What will it take for you to forget everything you saw here tonight?" he asked quietly, his voice steely, but did she detect a tiny bit of desperation in there, too?

Lucille held back another laugh. Now he was on the defensive. She moved in closer, much closer. When she was an inch away from his mouth, she whispered, "I have no intention of telling anyone anything if you don't."

Then she kissed him. Maybe she wanted him to forget about the things she herself had over shared. Maybe it was her boredom and unquenchable thirst for adventure. She didn't think it was because she found him irresistibly attractive, although that attraction was undeniably there.

She leaned back to break the kiss and he followed, keeping their mouths pressed together. His hand reached up to cup her face, her hands landed on his hips as she walked him backward until he hit the wall. He groaned and she pressed in closer, pushing, grinding into him. Noah's lips opened beneath hers, and she moved in, practically devouring him in intense, raging lust.

After much longer than Lucille had ever intended, she pushed back. She was breathing heavily, and so was Noah. He sagged against the wall, his black hair mussed from her hands, his suit distinctly rumbled. Lucille smoothed down her clothes, hoping she didn't look as messy as he did.

"You are incredibly infuriating, Lucille Anton," Noah said when he caught his breath.

Lucille snorted lightly. "So are you, Noah Harkin."

With that, she left, determined not to see the hot, irritating PI again. And she didn't. Not until a month later when she found him holding a conference in a linen closet at a fake sex party with Michel Polce and JP Tanaka. And now he worked for Simon and, by extension, for her. The very definition of complicated.

Chapter Five

Lucille's office suited her. She'd turned the smallest bedroom in her new condo into her haven of productivity. White with gold accents, a glass desk, all her devices in charging stations so she could catch up on the latest trending stories while simultaneously respond to emails and return phone calls all at the same time. She had her speakers set how she liked them and a mug warmer for her coffee. Her office was perfect. The cold bar stool she currently perched on in Simon's kitchen was a far cry from perfect.

She shifted, her muscles protesting the movement. Over the last few hours, she'd powered through Jasmine's defense. Her arguments for the school administration, multiple press releases, depending on how the school handled the incident, messages for her fans, statements for her to give the media, a folder of photos approved and formatted.

They were ready. Now, though, the late night and lack of sleep were catching up to her.

Lucille took a sip of her coffee and grimaced. Cold. Cold milk foam and beneath that tepid coffee. "This is when I need an assistant," she said, dumping the offensive liquid down the sink. But Lucille wasn't going to get an assistant. She didn't need another person in her business. There were already a few too many people in the know for her liking. Still, the assistant could be sent out to get fresh lattes, and wasn't that worth everything?

What she needed was for Simon to set up a place for her to work. Especially if she was going to get called halfway across the state every week to help him and Noah deal with whatever bone-headed decisions they decided to make next.

"Is something wrong?"

Lucille looked up as JP Tanaka wandered into the kitchen. The house was technically JP's, but when Simon moved in a few weeks ago, he'd wasted no time making it his own—a mix of art deco and contemporary avant-garde. JP didn't seem to mind.

Where Simon had an opinion on everything and everyone and made his living lying to all of the above, JP was more normal. Well, as normal as the co-CEO of a multi-billion-dollar tech company could be.

Lucille was about to answer his question when she noticed his askew tie. JP was, in his heart of hearts, an anxious nerd whose clothes always seemed to be fighting him. She slid off the stool and walked around the counter to him as he poured coffee out of the carafe. "Oh, it's nothing. Mind if I fix your tie? It's gone a little sideways."

JP looked down and sighed. "Yes, please. Damn thing never wants to behave when I need it to."

Lucille straightened it and then his suit jacket. "Big meeting today?" she asked, indicating the outfit. JP didn't dress up unless forced, unlike Simon who never turned down the chance to dress his best.

JP sighed again. "Unfortunately, yes. Investors or something."

Lucille went back to her uncomfortable stool.

"Do I even want to ask what you all were up to last night?"

Lucille met JP's wary gaze. He didn't exactly disapprove of their business, but he also didn't fully approve either. Simon said it was because JP was a far better human being than they were and Lucille agreed. "You do not," she replied with a smile.

JP nodded. "Any idea where Simon went off to? He wasn't here when I woke up."

"He said, and I quote, 'I have some things to take care of. Be back later, Luce.'"

"Cryptic."

"Indeed."

They chatted for a few more minutes. JP had been Lucille's client when she worked for the PR agency, and he'd remained her friend after she quit to rejoin the spin doctor team.

"When do you fly back?" JP asked. He sat at the stool next to her, eating cereal and keeping a careful eye on the clock.

"In a few hours." She'd wanted to be gone first thing in the morning, but since they still hadn't gotten a company jet, she was forced to adhere to commercial airline availabilities and timelines.

"That's too bad," JP said with a frown. He carried his bowl over to the sink, rinsed it out, and put it in the dishwasher before explaining himself. "I feel like we never see each other these days."

Lucille smiled. It hadn't been so long ago she hadn't had anyone in her life, and now there were people who wanted to spend time with her. Surreal.

She promised to visit again soon, and JP rushed out the door, forgot his shoulder bag, and came back in to get it.

JP and Simon were so different in so many ways and yet they worked.

Her mind wandered to the thoughts she didn't want to think. To the relationship she didn't want to want. JP was a good fit for Simon, but she wanted, no needed, something different. She needed someone who could keep up with her, someone smart but who also had a great body and who could keep her on her toes. The only person she'd met who had all of those qualities was, unfortunately, Noah Harkin, and he had the atrocious character flaw of being unbearable.

Her phone dinged. She glanced down at it and saw Simon's name on the screen. When he'd left, he'd said it was far too early to discuss Noah's inability to be flexible with the plan or Lucille's refusal to engage in any more of his late-night escapades. Apparently, now he was ready.

Simon's text read *Oh, please, like you didn't have fun.*

Playing look out for Noah Harkin and then being stranded with the selfsame Mr. Harkin because you

*forgot where the rendezvous point was? No, I did not
have fun.*

She had enjoyed on their previous hare-brained
missions. Stealing Sylvia's expensive gown and rescuing Michel and Brett. Dressing up and crashing the Deviant Club party, even though it turned
out not to be a party and not the Deviant Club.
Last night was too planned, too predictable, and it
had ended with too much unnecessary kissing. She
wasn't telling Simon about that. He didn't need any
more ammo in his campaign to get her to accept
Noah.

She turned back to the email, from one of her
newer clients, a YouTube star who'd accidentally uploaded some embarrassing footage he hadn't
meant to. Lucille had gotten the footage off the
channel and released a report that the star's channel
had been hacked and viciously attacked. There was
an outpouring of support from his fans, some skep-
ticism from the people who post nasty comments at
every opportunity, and the thing was blowing over.

The email was a thank-you. Lucille smiled as
she read. She hoped he wouldn't be a client for
long. Normally, she didn't even work with celebrities
who'd had a onetime screwup. They were far more
likely to learn their lesson and change, thereby not

needing her services on a long-term basis. They didn't bring in the money like her repeat clients. But she'd sympathized with this kid and this time, she honestly hoped she wouldn't hear from him again.

That's not what I saw.

She'd been determined to ignore further texts from Simon. There were a dozen more messages in her inbox and the rest weren't likely to be happy resolutions or thank-you notes. Yet, she was drawn to her phone and read the new text before she could stop herself. And then read it again.

It could mean one of two things. Either Simon knew she and Noah kissed or he suspected and wanted to trick her into confessing. A ploy that might work on others, but she knew all Simon's moves—he'd taught them to her. So instead of playing, she changed the subject.

What ever happened with Mimi Richards? I have a return to sender message from her publicist.

Don't change the subject on me, Lucy. Were you or were you not making out with Noah last night?

She wasn't taking the bait. Besides, she honestly did need to know what had happened with Mimi. Mimi Richards was one of about ten clients she'd worked with for years but who now had either changed their email address or phone number or both and were proving challenging to get in touch with. Were they mad at her for leaving the business and moving to San Francisco? Not possible since almost no one knew she'd done that. These were not celebrities who were getting help elsewhere or who had fallen out of the public eye. The entertainment news was still full of them, their shows were still on the air, and they had tours booked. Which only left the explanation that, during her absence, Simon had somehow managed to chase away her clientele, some of them so thoroughly that they weren't willing to come back now she was in charge again.

No. Don't YOU change the subject. What happened with Mimi??

There was a lag before Simon's reply came. While she waited, she clicked on the next message. It was from a PA who used to work for a client of hers and who now seemed to have another employer in trouble. The message ran:

Hi Lucille,

I hear you're back and I could not be more relieved. You no doubt heard about Raphael's retirement? Well, since he no longer needs me, I've started working for a producer by the name of Lora Crescent. She has taken up some...activities and has recently had some near misses. She asked me to find her a better publicist and I, naturally, contacted you. I would like to set up a meeting between you and Lora soon because she desperately needs to keep this under the radar. She has an award contender coming out in a few months and the film cannot handle any kind of bad publicity.

Thank you,

Pia

Lucille reached for her mug before remembering that she'd left it in the sink, and scowled. This was the ideal moment to take a sip of a coffee and then begin furiously typing out a response. In the absence of a beverage, she was forced to sit and ponder instead. If she was going to have that assistant, that mythical assistant who kept the coffee hot and flowing, she would hire Pia in a heartbeat. The woman was efficient, organized, discreet, and astronomically expensive. Which was why so many of her clients were also Lucille's clients. Someday, maybe, Lucille could lure her away from the front lines of celebrity life and into the spin doctor business. Not if Simon kept losing all her clients, of course.

Her phone buzzed. Simon finally replied to her question.

We had a difference of opinion.

Which was?

Did you know she was Cooper's cousin? She thought I killed him and I told her I didn't. It did not end well.

One would think that, in the celebrity spin doctor business of all places, things like false murder charges and years spent as a fugitive wouldn't matter to those who were shelling out money to cover up their dirty secrets. And yet it was human nature to put on aspirations of morality while doing Lord knew what yourself. At least, it was the nature of many of their clients and it was deeply obnoxious.

Lucille felt a wave of protectiveness and indignation. *That bitch.*

Sorry I've lost you so many clients, Lucy.

She couldn't be mad at him, not when he would never intentionally hurt the business, his business, his life's work. If it hadn't been for the incident eight years ago involving the Deviant Club, an incriminating tape, and the murder of the club president, a murder Simon was falsely accused of, none of these clients would have left. Lucille had long since forgiven Simon's mistakes from that time. Having a family member, one she loved, was far more important than holding a grudge over him fleeing wrongful imprisonment. She was mad at the clients who wouldn't give Simon another chance, not after he gave so much of his time and energy to rescuing their second chances.

It's ok. We'll bounce back. We always do.

She wouldn't tell him about the prospective client, nor did she tell him about Jasmine or the other two clients she'd gotten the day before through some of her PR contacts. Word was circulating that Lucille was back and soon this slow period would end. But she wasn't going to tell Simon anything more than he needed to know. It was one of the most important rules of celebrity spin doctors—never tell the people you love what you're up to.

We already are thanks to Noah.

Lucille rolled her eyes. She knew it had more to do with Simon being in a new city with a whole different type of clientele than because Noah had been working with him for the past few weeks. Also, Simon having an insanely rich boyfriend probably didn't hurt things.

Keep telling yourself that.

She put her phone down, replied to Pia, replied to a couple of current clients, drafted a contract, and drafted four short breaking-news stories that she then passed through a series of fake accounts to the various media outlets. Their whole computer system was run on a server with the security of the Pentagon and stored by LT Tech. JP was, so far, the only person who'd traced their account to his company and then spent a good hour explaining how the data was encrypted and archived, during which Lucille seriously questioned all the decisions she'd made in life that had led her to that point.

Her phone alarm went off. Time to leave for the airport.

Then her phone rang. She hoped against hope it wasn't Noah. It wasn't. It was Simon. Simon, who hadn't responded to her snark, who said phone calls were relics of a bygone era and would only video chat. Simon was calling her.

"Yes?" she said by way of a greeting. Normally, with her clients, she pretended she couldn't see the caller ID and always answered in a professional, guarded tone. She was too impatient to know what was happening to give her uncle the same treatment.

There was a pause on the other end of the line. Then Simon said, in a cautious voice that didn't sound like him at all, "Lucy, are you still at my house?"

"Oh, my God. What happened?" She couldn't contain herself. She hadn't experienced a rush of fear this intense since she saw Simon being arrested by her ex-boyfriend over eight years ago.

"Why do you assume something happened?" Simon said, his voice back to its usual casual charm. A game.

"Simon. You're calling me. Not video calling, not texting, not emailing. Calling. You don't call. In fact, the last time you called me was the day my mother got arrested again and you were calling to find out when our custody court hearing was," she explained, trying to keep her voice calm and not jump immediately to the conclusion that the police had found a loophole and arrested Simon for the murder that he was never officially cleared of and that he was calling from prison.

"Ah, right. I see how that's alarming," said Simon. There was some noise at his end, voices in the background speaking too quietly for her to hear what they said.

"Is someone else there? You are in prison, aren't you? Tell me right now if you are because this time, I won't be the only person who kills you if you disappear without a word. I know JP will help me, and I'm sure he has contacts who can make sure no one knows where we hide your body."

"What? Jesus. Have you talked about this?"

Lucille hesitated. She opted not to tell Simon one way or the other. *Let him stew on that.* "Not important. Answer my question, Uncle Simon."

"I'm not in prison. And your pause confirmed it. You and JP have talked about what you'll do if I disappear again." Lucille couldn't tell exactly, but he sounded annoyed and disbelieving. About her, JP, or both?

"We have to have a plan, just in case," she said, quoting Simon's words from her spin doctor training back to him.

"Fair enough," he agreed, "In a weird way, it's kind of sweet that you two love me so much you'd hunt me down and kill me if I break your hearts again."

"Weird? I think you mean fucked up." She tried to hold back the desire to scream at him to explain himself.

Simon chuckled. Then he sighed. "Okay, so it's nothing like that. It's actually nothing I did...directly...for once."

Lucille waited, the jury still out on whether the day would end in homicide.

"Noah has taken on his first client. It's a good case, lots of potential for long-term cash flow, all that stuff. And interesting too. Lots of reputation work to do."

There was a catch. The other shoe was about to drop, and she wasn't going to reply until it did. Simon was hedging around the topic, not telling her the big, important part of it.

"All in all, I think it's a good case for him. He's definitely ready. I mean, we knew he had the training and, while he does lack somewhat in flexibility, I'm positive he'll adjust after working with us for longer. Pity you two can't get over your unnecessary animosity and get along better."

"Simon. Tell me who the fucking client is."

"I will. But you're going to want to cancel your flight. This might take a while. I'm on my way back to the house right now so we can talk in person."

Lucille hated this more and more. "Simon," she growled.

There was a pause. A long pause. Lucille checked to see if they were still connected. They were. She waited.

Finally, Simon spoke. "It's Sylvia. She's out of wherever she was, rehab, I think, and is back. Noah's new client is Sylvia Stanton."

CHAPTER SIX

To the casual third-party observer, Brett's reaction upon opening the door and discovering his older sister on the other side was probably deeply comical. To him, there was nothing funny about finding a family member, his family member, outside his room. He jerked backward, his eyes widened, his mouth fell open, and he could swear his heart stopped. Then he hissed, "Patience?" and resisted the urge to poke her to see if she was real.

"Brett. I thought that was you in the lobby but didn't understand why you'd be here of all places. Good. Now you can explain yourself." Patience Jacobs was a straightforward person, always had been. As a sibling, she was brutally honest, especially when she was drinking, and she was frequently drinking.

Shorter than Brett, she wore tall platform sandals that put them at eye level. She wore a stereotypical tropical tourist outfit, a sarong wrapped into a halter-neck dress, gaping open in places to reveal her bikini underneath. Her hair was in two braids and she had a huge flower behind one ear. In her hands, with their stubby, bitten nails, was a coconut with a straw and a little umbrella sticking out of it. In features, she and Brett had always looked alike, same brown hair, same blue eyes, same angular facial structure. But physical features were where their similarities stopped, or at least Brett had always desperately hoped that was the case.

"Explain myself?" Brett echoed because he couldn't think of anything else to say.

"Yes." That was all he would get from Patience. She didn't expand on her statements, had never felt the need to. Her writing matched her elocution—brief, heavily punctuated, and direct. Her characters always sounded like miniature versions of herself, only marginally less horrible. "What the fuck is wrong with your room?"

Before he could answer, a noise from the bedroom reminded Brett he wasn't alone. Michel was in the bedroom. Michel, who could walk out at any moment wearing who knew what. Considering where their last interaction had almost gone, it wouldn't be out of the question for Michel to strut in in the buff. Or in his tiny Speedo...

He had to get his sister out of there. Now.

"Who's your traveling companion?" Of course, Patience knew he hadn't come alone. If she'd seen Brett, she'd doubtless seen Michel, too.

Brett proceeded carefully, sure the only thing protecting him now was the hope Patience hadn't recognized Michel. "Um...that's my friend. We're here on some business."

Patience didn't react. She took a long sip of whatever she was drinking out of the coconut and continued to stare at Brett. Finally, she said, "Friends, huh? Is that what we're calling it these days?"

Brett felt his face grow hot. He didn't know how his family would respond to him being bi. It had never come up before. He'd assumed they wouldn't care, just like they didn't care about the rest of his life. Patience, for all her bluntness, was hard to read. She might be messing with him, but Brett had never known her to have a sense of humor. Was she pissed at him for not telling the family about his new boyfriend? Or about the trip to the island? Or, slim chance though it was, could she be happy to see him?

"Just...give me a second," Brett said. He closed the door and sprinted to the bedroom.

Michel stood by the bed, contemplating his open suitcase, his jacket discarded on a nearby chair and his shirt unbuttoned to reveal his muscular chest. Brett made an involuntary sound as his extinguished lust rushed back.

"Brett? Are you okay?" Michel moved around the bed and stood before him, rubbing his arms in a way that was both comforting and distracting.

"My sister's here," Brett choked out.

Michel's hands froze. "Which sister?"

"Patience."

Michel nodded, seeming relieved.

"But..." Brett continued, the thought occurring to him as he spoke. "She didn't say she was alone. There's a good chance she's not."

The frown that had started with the mention of his sister deepened on Michel's face.

Brett hurried through the rest. "She didn't seem to know you're here. She knows I'm here with someone but didn't say anything about you. I'll go with Patience right now, find out what she's up to, and be back as soon as I can. With any luck, she's alone and leaving tomorrow."

"Okay..." Michel said, clearly unconvinced. "Then we can continue where we left off?"

Brett tried to determine what was causing him more anxiety, the presence of his sisters or the impending intimacy with Michel. He nodded.

Michel smiled, but it was a small, unsure one. He was worried too, but whether it was about Brett's meddling, his destructive siblings, or his weird reaction, Brett didn't want to ask.

He gently pulled out of Michel's grasp and left the room. The hope that Patience had been a mirage and the hall would be empty was futile. His sister waited for him just outside the door. "Let's go downstairs," he said briskly and led the way. It wasn't until he reached the first floor that he realized he hadn't kissed Michel when he'd left.

In an empty alcove in the main lobby, Brett sat down on an uncomfortable tropical print ottoman and waved for Patience to take the chair across from him.

"That was odd, even for you," Patience said as she settled herself into the chair. She crossed one leg over the other, her sarong thankfully wrapping more around her body.

"What are you doing here, Patience?" Brett asked in a low voice. He'd been trying to think of what to say the whole way down. Did he want her to leave? Or just leave him alone? He was fairly certain he didn't want to know how the rest of his family were doing. He was absolutely certain he didn't want her to know he was there with Michel.

Patience shook her head. "That's not how it works. I asked you first. I found you. You wouldn't even be in a position to ask me that question if I hadn't."

Brett took a deep breath. His jaw clenched, but he didn't look away. Not making eye contact was a sign of weakness to predators and the Jacobs family. "I'm here on vacation with a friend. I had some time off from work, and Uncle Lou was able to book me a spot."

"Funny," Patience began, pausing to take a drink. "Uncle Lou didn't mention you were coming to The Reef."

Uncle Lou was Lou Stanton, owner and CEO of Stanton Enterprises, father to Sylvia Stanton, and their mother's brother. He was obscenely rich, obscenely powerful, and rather a pill. Brett avoided him at all costs and it seemed to be the best way to have a relationship with the man. Lou Stanton owned Mino Island, but he also had connections just about everywhere, including the secret, exclusive Reef resort. Should Patience decide to ask Uncle

Lou about Brett, he could easily find the reservation under Michel's name and this vacation, not to mention the privacy of their relationship, would be over. It all depended on Brett keeping his story, his life, so unbelievably dull that Patience wouldn't be tempted to follow up. Tenuous and not a little bit terrifying.

"No, he must not have put it together that we'd be here at the same time. Besides, I booked through my work, LT Technologies," Brett said, contradicting himself and wondering if his astute sister would notice.

Patience sat back in her chair, the flicker of keen interest dying. "Oh, right, remind me what you do again?"

Gladly, Brett thought and launched into an explanation of his research. It had always been his number one defense against his family—talking about the experiments he was conducting in such details that their eyes glazed over and they forgot why they'd wanted to spend time with him in the first place. Well, apart from that period when he'd tried to be a screenwriter, play by their rules, and win their affection. It had worked for a while, then led to some of the darkest days of his life. If it hadn't been for Lucille and Michel, he'd still be face down in a pile of unwashed sheets and dirty dishes.

Sure enough, Patience cut him off partway through his explanation of the chemical composition of various components of their new cellular technologies. She stood up. "I regret asking. And my drink's empty. We're going to the bar."

Brett didn't want to go to the bar. He drank so infrequently now and he didn't want to waste that infrequency on drinks with his sister. It sounded cruel, even when he said it to himself, but he had the deep psychological wounds to show what bonding with his family led to. Yet, he stood, followed her across the lobby, and out the doors leading to the pool and the poolside cantina.

"You still didn't explain why you're here," Brett said as he scanned the sunbathers, checking to see how extensive the relative ambush was. He recognized a few of his fellow guests as people he'd met when he used to attend Hollywood parties, no familial relations. His gaze snagged on a woman sitting by herself at a high top on the other side of the pool. He knew her. Didn't he? She seemed so familiar...

"Evelyn. I was right, it was Brett." Patience interrupted his thoughts. As he processed her words, his stomach sank and he turned to face another woman, this one well known to him, unfortunately.

She used to have the same hair as Brett and Patience. Brown as brown can be. But for as long as Brett could remember, she'd worn it deep red, and while the rest of the family generally opted for the unkempt, wild look of the artist, Evelyn Jacobs went sleek and styled with carefully controlled waves. She turned on her heels, whipping her hair over her shoulder, and fixed Brett with the full force of her smoky-eyed gaze.

She was wearing a dress with Michel's face on it. Not a single image either. Oh no, the dress was covered in photos of Michel. They were from his coffee table book—him shirtless and brooding, looking away from the camera. Michel gazing directly at the viewer, his eyes smoldering. Michel leaning casually against the counter in his mansion, his shirt unbuttoned and his posture relaxed. Michel sitting by a creek with a guitar. Every inch the tortured, genius artist the Jacobs family loved. There was no way he could allow them anywhere near Michel, not now, not ever.

When Evelyn saw him, she stopped drinking from the floral print paper straw that stuck out of her goblet-sized margarita. After a moment in which she seemed to be deciding how to react to his presence, she opened her arms and said, "Bretty," in a high voice, filled with fake excitement.

"Hey Evie," he said, using her old nickname in response to his own. He stepped toward her and returned her weak hug with a quick back pat before retreating to a safe distance and hiding his cringe at her outfit.

Brett was torn between not knowing what to say and not knowing how to react. He hadn't seen his sisters in nearly two years, ever since his writer's block over his second script and Michel's perceived abandonment caused him to retreat into a hole of depression, shame, and alcoholism.

Patience ordered another coconut and raised her eyebrows at Brett to ask if he wanted anything.

"No," he said, shaking his head. "I don't drink much anymore."

His sisters exchanged a look. "Hmm." Patience smiled when the bartender handed her the drink.

Evelyn cut into the awkward silence. "Did Patience tell you why we're here? Uncle Lou wants to turn her series into a TV show for his new streaming service. Patience, being the shrewd businesswoman she is, wasn't going to just sign any old offer simply because he's our uncle. So, he flew us out here for a few days to sweeten the deal."

Brett's blood froze. "Uncle Lou is here?" There went his cover story, and he hadn't even had the chance to perfect it.

Evelyn smacked his arm. She'd always reminded him of the first sorority girl to get drunk at the party. "Don't be ridiculous. Of course, Uncle Lou doesn't have the time to jet off to an island."

Patience shot Brett a look that he didn't understand but immediately assumed meant she was onto him because why wouldn't he suddenly develop a persecution complex? She led the way to one of the high tops near the pool.

While his siblings bent over their tropical beverages, Brett leaned back, folded his arms, and tried to keep himself from running away screaming. It wasn't like he was going to hang out with them all day, but he did need to get some info. Like what they'd be doing for the next few days so Michel and he could avoid them. He looked at Evelyn's dress again and bit back his commentary.

It wasn't just that his family was obsessed with this heavy drinking, destructively creative lifestyle. Nor that they were entirely focused on money and careers and getting ahead in the business. If those flaws were the worst of them, Brett would have begged Michel to come with him as emotional support. But no, the real problem was right there on that damn dress. Evelyn Louise Jacobs was the president of the largest and most active Michel Polce fan club in the world. They had weekly meetings, they went to all his appearances, and they had just about every piece of clothing autographed they could. There were forums, groups on every social media platform, and a physical headquarters, the location of which was the worst kept secret in LA. More than a few of them walked the fine line between fandom and obsession.

It was only a matter of time before the fan club found out about his and Michel's relationship. They knew he was friends with Michel, but Brett had always been able to downplay their connection. If they knew he was dating the man and totally in love... well, when that truth came out, Brett had no illusions he'd ever be invited back into the family circle. He'd heard what Evelyn had said about Sylvia, and she was their cousin. Her own brother? He knew his tenuous relationship with his siblings wouldn't survive the news and didn't want to be anywhere in the vicinity when it exploded.

Evelyn jumped in before he could ask about their plans.

"What are you doing here, Bretty? Did Uncle Lou invite you, too? He really should have told us if he did."

Patience answered, her eyes boring into Brett as she did. "No, Brett's here on a vacation with a friend."

"Ooh, *a friend*. What's that code for? A girlfriend?" Evelyn might have been teasing, but her voice was sharp, laced with something more than idle curiosity, and it cut at Brett.

Brett wanted to say it was none of her damn business if he had a girlfriend, or a boyfriend for that matter. Instead, he changed the subject. "So, what're you two up to while you're here for the next..."

He trailed off, hoping one of them would tell them exactly how long they were staying.

"Two days," Patience said. "You're looking at it," she added.

Evelyn nodded. "Yep. Two more days of relaxing with absolutely nothing to do. I've told the club I'm completely unavailable, and Patience isn't taking calls from her agent or publisher right now. A complete disconnect."

"Sounds wonderful," Brett said and meant it. He let them chatter on, asking questions now and again about Patience's latest work and the rest of the family. He didn't inquire about the fan club, although

Evelyn filled him in anyway. It wasn't until the sun was setting and he realized he was starving that he broke away from them. They both encouraged him to join them for dinner and to bring his friend, but he claimed jetlag and headed toward the room. He hadn't meant linger for so long but also hadn't been able to bring himself to leave. Was he really so worried about what they'd get up to if he wasn't watching? Or was there something else, some deep-seated fear of leaning into this intimate vacation with Michel that kept him away? Brett pushed the second option aside as utter nonsense. He wasn't afraid of being with Michel. His reticence had everything to do with his terrible sisters and their potential to ruin his vacation.

CHAPTER SEVEN

Lucille sat at the island in Simon's kitchen and seethed. Simon had said he'd be back soon, and she suspected he dragged his feet to avoid her ire. She didn't blame him, even though she'd canceled her flight for him. If she was in his place and had made a deal with the devil, she'd be avoiding him. Sure, it was Noah who'd made the deal but, in Lucille's mind as she stewed, that was at most a semantic distinction.

Meanwhile, based on the frantic texts she'd been getting, her ex-boyfriend/best friend was having his own family crisis. What was with the Stanton-Jacobs family, and why did they all have to be so dramatic? She hoped Brett and Michel had some kids so they could start a new branch of the family that was less destructive and murderous. Not necessarily more stable, given Michel's obsessive nature and Brett's family history of alcoholism, but one that didn't pride itself on how many people's lives they could rip apart.

To take her mind off her blinding rage, she replied to Brett's plea for advice.

Under no circumstances should you let Michel anywhere near your sisters!

Brett responded immediately. *Obviously. We've agreed on that. What else you got?*

Can you knock them unconscious or drug them for a few days? Lock them in their room?

There was a pause. Lucille wondered if Brett was seriously considering her suggestions. *Unlikely. They're both strong and Patience would see through any trap I come up with.*

Only one other option—you and Michel will have to stay in the room for days, just constantly having sex.

He ignored that suggestion completely. *I'm exploring options for us to get away from the hotel.*

Lucille wanted to bang her head against the marble countertop at the extreme cluelessness of the men in her life. She didn't have time to delve into Brett's self-doubt where his hot new boyfriend was concerned, but she was absolutely certain Michel would be into a sex marathon, even without the family avoidance excuse. She tried another tactic.

Wouldn't you rather have a sex marathon?

Another pause. *I mean, sure, yeah. But we'd be too easy to track down if we stayed in the room. Any other ideas?*

Lucille didn't like the tone of his text. If she were his therapist, she'd say he was deflecting his fears about not being enough for Michel and lashing out at her instead of admitting his feelings. But she wasn't his therapist. She was his ex-girlfriend, and dammit, she had shit to take care of. Brett was going to have to work through this himself.

So, she did what she'd do for any other client. She told him what he wanted to hear.

Here's what you do. I've never been to Reef, but I assume, since it's a resort island, there's a waterfall somewhere. Get some food, a map, and take Michel on a hike to said waterfall. Make sure the whole thing is romantic as fuck and don't get back to the hotel until sunset, got it?

Um...hiking? Have you ever seen Michel go hiking? Or me??

Exactly. It's unexpected. No one will look for you.

Ok...

Stop complaining and just do it.

Fine.

Lucille put down her phone with a sigh. It was Brett's fault if he let his anxiety and irrational worries get the better of him. And yet, she felt responsible. She was rooting for Brett and Michel. They were great together, and she hoped Brett would get his head out of his ass soon enough to notice.

A car pulled into the driveway. She set aside Brett's troubles and put on her game face, the one she reserved for dealing with her uncle.

The front door opened and closed. Footsteps in the hall, and then Simon strolled into the kitchen. Lucille saw him from the corner of her eye but didn't look up from her tablet. She scrolled through a news story she was pretending to read.

"Good morning, Lucy," Simon said, his voice breezy and light.

Lucille set her tablet down slowly. Equally slowly, she turned her head toward Simon to find him examining a nonexistent spot on his lavender suit jacket. Only four years her senior, Simon was her match in build, in attitude, and in impeccable style. They differed in coloring—Lucille being a brown-eyed brunette while Simon had blue eyes, silvery blond hair, and a majestic fake tan.

She took a deep, audible breath. "Simon. What the fuck."

If Simon was put off by her tone, he didn't show it. It was the Anton way. Speak emotions with words but don't show the emotion in facial expression or body language. The effect was powerful and disarming and worked on everyone. Everyone, that was, who wasn't also an Anton.

"Would you like some wine?" Simon asked, looking up and walking into the kitchen area. The house was an open floor plan, which Simon probably hated, but had a grand, art deco style that he probably loved. "JP has terrible taste in wine, bless him, but I've been steadily rectifying that."

The redirect. A classic Simon move.

"Simon," Lucille said.

He continued. "It feels more like a white day than a red. Honestly, I'd say that about all the days in LA, but up here it's much harder to distinguish. Certainly not rose season, whatever those trend followers say. Like excuse me, what are you? An influencer? Well, if that's the case, use your influence for something other than getting everyone to drink rose."

Yet another tactic—acting like a flamboyant gay stereotype in order to get people to laugh and dismiss him.

"Simon," Lucille said again. She hadn't moved from her bar stool and hadn't turned her glare from Simon, who was leaning over the wine fridge and touching bottles as he spoke.

"You know, I think Noah's going to be back any moment. What did he say last night that got you so worked up?"

And finally, bring up another emotionally charged topic, one she'd be tempted to engage on. Simon was throwing all the tricks in the spin doctor handbook at her, which meant he didn't want to admit he'd fucked up, but he had, definitely, fucked up.

Lucille leaned forward on the white marble-topped island, looking down at Simon with her sternest look. "I know all your tricks, remember? I can see right through you. Your games are my games. So, do us both a favor, cut the bullshit, and tell me why the hell you'd think working with Sylvia Stanton is a good idea."

Simon rose slowly, a bottle of wine in his hand. When he looked at Lucille, his face was calm. Not open, but not a mask either, a quiet neutral. "Do you still want the wine?" he asked softly.

Lucille nodded. "We're going to need lots of wine."

Simon sighed as he hunted for a corkscrew. "It wasn't my idea to work with her. But it's the first client Noah's gotten on his own and he seemed so determined that he could do something for her. I don't know."

"Don't you dare tell me he thinks she's changed."

Simon snorted. "Even he wouldn't go that far. But I know, and you know, she's profitable and has a lot of long-term potential."

It was Lucille's turn to scoff.

"Now, Lucy, don't let your personal feelings get in the way of business."

Lucille accepted the glass of wine he passed to her. "That rule stopped working when we started having relationships with our clients," she said harshly.

"True. Brett was, and always will be, a terrible mistake," Simon said, sipping his wine.

Lucille clenched her jaw and set her glass down on the counter harder than she meant to. "This has nothing to do with Brett and you know it. In case you've forgotten, it wasn't only Brett Sylvia tried to kill."

"I remember."

"Then why, Simon? Why are you willing to take a risk on Sylvia knowing full well she could ruin everything we've spent the last few months trying to piece back together?" Lucille kept her voice steady, but she didn't feel steady in the least. The last time Simon had gambled on his clients, it had led to her being abandoned for eight years, not knowing if he was alive or dead.

Before Simon could answer her question, the front door opened and Noah entered. He wore a black leather jacket, tight jeans, and a V-neck t-shirt. The whole effect was very *Rebel Without A Cause*, and Lucille wouldn't have been surprised to see an unlit cigarette dangling from the edge of his mouth. Which led her to thinking about his mouth and kissing him, and about how those clothes were so tight they left nothing to the imagination.

Not the time.

Noah stopped when he saw Lucille. An expression of something like pleasant surprise crossed his face but was swiftly replaced with a frown. "Lucille. What are you still doing here?"

Noah didn't know it was the wrong thing to say. Anything he said at the moment was the wrong thing, but Lucille sure as hell wasn't going to tell him that. Besides, whatever the fuck Noah was dressed up to be, he looked stupid, which only further proved that he made terrible choices.

"Lucy's got a bone to pick with you about your new client," Simon said, calmly, swirling the wine around his glass like he was barely interested in what transpired. Like she hadn't just been laying into him with equal fervor.

"Lucy can speak for herself, thank you." She was annoyed to hear her words come out in a growl. "What the fuck were you thinking? Sylvia Stanton?" She turned the full force of her anger on Noah and was pleased to see him take a step back.

"Whoa," he said, putting his hands up. "What's all this about?"

Lucille looked at him like he couldn't possibly be that dense. She was fantastic at reading people and was surprised to find that Noah's shock was genuine. He blinked back at her like he had no idea what brought on this fury, and it seemed he really didn't.

"You didn't tell him?" she threw back at Simon.

Simon sighed. "Lucy, that was all a long time ago."

"It was six months ago."

Simon shrugged. "Right, well, it didn't seem like my story to tell."

She narrowed her eyes at him. "Bullshit. You want to work with her, don't you?"

Here, Noah cut in again. "Why wouldn't he? She's insanely rich, screams drama, and has zero scruples. I'd say she's exactly what we want in a client."

Lucille heard Noah but didn't take her eyes off her uncle, who was busy studying his glass intensely. "He's right, isn't he?" she asked him softly, her voice venomous. "You wanted to see if you could do it. If you could spin Sylvia Stanton into a semi-respectable celebrity."

Simon finally looked up and met her gaze. "Yes," was all he said. No spin, no games, no defection. The simple, honest truth.

Lucille blinked. It was the only response that could deflate her. She knew the Anton games, the rules, the avoidances. But the truth? That she had no defenses against. "Fine," she said.

Noah had walked over to the counter during this interchange and stood at the end, in between Lucille and Simon. He looked at Lucille. "I take it you don't like her?"

She might not be completely livid with Noah anymore, but she wasn't going to suddenly start being sweet to him. That would imply liking and feelings, and Lucille was in no mood to have those. "Obviously, I don't like her. And I wouldn't put it past you to work with her just because you knew it annoyed me."

Noah accepted the glass of wine Simon slid to him. "Thanks. You know, I absolutely would do that, but I'm afraid, this time, I didn't. I happened to be sitting near her in a restaurant and overheard her talking to someone about her ruined reputation and how she'd do anything to get her old life back."

Lucille scoffed. "Right. And you suggested a total personality makeover?"

Simon laughed. "I don't think even that would be enough, Lucy."

"I haven't suggested anything yet. I haven't even met with her, I just told her I could help and to give me a call. I think she's going back to LA tonight, so I'll be in your area," Noah said. His tone was matter-of-fact, giving her no indication of what he personally thought of being in the same city as her for another day.

"And what, you want my help?" Lucille didn't try to keep the disdain out of her voice.

"Lucy," Simon said with a warning note.

"Don't you Lucy me, Uncle Simon," Lucille said, standing and packing up her bag. "I will do a lot for this business. I have done a lot for this business. But one thing I won't do is work with Sylvia Stanton."

"Did I ask for your help?" Noah shot back. "I'm perfectly capable of handling a client on my own. It's not like a ran my own PI business for years or anything. I'm here for the same reason you're both here. I got tired of working alone."

Lucille seethed.

Simon laughed softly. "Yes, it is much better to work with friends. So many more possibilities." He raised his glass in a toast.

Noah met the toast with a grin. "To new friends and new clients."

Lucille could see the moment both men noticed her fury. They set their glasses down. Simon became extremely interested in a painting on the wall. Noah met her glare, his jaw set, but without any fight in his eyes. If she didn't say something soon, he might try to explain his decision again. That she couldn't handle.

In her lowest, most dangerous voice, she said, "Don't pretend you know anything about me. And don't delude yourself for one second that you know a damn thing about Sylvia Stanton. She'll chew you up and spit you back out. And I'm not going to pick up the pieces this time."

With those parting shots, she marched out of the house. *Let them work out their problems themselves.* She had a premiere to attend.

CHAPTER EIGHT

Their room was positioned so the balcony was entirely hidden from prying eyes. In order to see inside, a person would either have to be stuck to the wall between the balcony and the next room or navigate the rocks and dense shrubbery below. Even the roof was designed so that it'd be impossible for anyone to peer over the edge without themselves being seen. When The Reef promised privacy, they delivered.

It only was after Brett had scoped all these possibilities and triple-checked the lock on the door that he finally focused on the dinner before him.

The sun was setting over the water, the air was warm but cooler than the heat of the day. Torches and candles deterred bugs from approaching the balcony. The clouds, barely present during the day, drifted lazily, tinged in purples and oranges, magical in their ethereal, slow journey across the sky. All around them was the scent of tropical air, pungent with flowers and sea salt, mixing with the rich aroma of their steak dinner.

Brett checked the door one last time, testing the chain for the fourth time in as many minutes. He was pretty sure his sisters wouldn't go to the extreme of breaking in from the outside to get to him, but he wouldn't put it past them to show up at his room and demand entry. No matter he hadn't spoken to them in years. No matter he was, for all intents and purposes, estranged from the family. They clearly wanted to pick up right where they'd left off with him and expected him to do the same.

And if Evelyn found out Michel was there? No amount of rocks or shrubbery would keep her out.

Brett hurried to the table just as Michel took his seat. Michel was devastating in the romantic glow of the candles. His hair was still wet from his shower, and he wore a soft-looking shirt unbuttoned at the top, showing off a tantalizing preview of bronzed skin.

Meanwhile, Brett wore his traveling clothes, having scrambled to get back to the room after leaving his sisters. When he'd arrived, Michel was waiting with a private dinner on the balcony and there was no way he was delaying their meal, even for the time it took to change his clothes.

If Michel noticed Brett still wore his t-shirt and jeans from the flight, even in the humid heat of the island, he didn't comment on it. All he said when Brett came back was, "Oh, good, I was afraid you'd miss dinner," and coupled it with a soft, delicious greeting kiss.

Brett felt tingly, both from the kiss and his rising anxiety. He wanted to tell Michel what happened with his sisters but dreaded bringing up the subject and ruining the ambiance. The indecision was stressing him the fuck out. And, there was also something else, something simmering below the surface and threatening to rear up and screw with his head.

With all the casual calm he could muster, he cut into the steak and asked Michel, "How was your afternoon? Did you go to the beach?"

Michel didn't say anything.

Brett looked up and met his frie—boyfriend's gaze. It was so new, so different to think of Michel as his boyfriend, the word didn't come naturally. Michel didn't seem disappointed or hurt, although he had every right to be after being ditched for hours. Rather, his expression was deep and longing, like he was gazing into Brett's soul. Brett felt the heat in that look and his body responded to it. It was intense, thrilling, terrifying, and so, so hot. He gulped from his water glass, hoping to temper the flames.

"Yes. It was everything a beach should be. Soft sand, cool water, and the sun shining down on it all."

Frequently, when Michel spoke, he could be reciting a poem or composing his memoirs. His voice ebbed and flowed and drew people in. He might be reading the most boring instructional manual in the world and his recitation would still make a listener salivate.

"That sounds lovely," Brett choked out.

A silence fell between them, shimmering with tension and, on Brett's side, panic. He stared down at his plate, moved a potato around with his fork, and tried not to hyperventilate and ruin the mood.

Michel's hand covered his, stopping the listless potato maneuvering. Setting his fork down, Brett laced his fingers with Michel's. It helped. "I don't want to talk about my sisters," Brett said heavily, "I'm sorry I couldn't get away from them sooner and join you at the beach. And that I was almost late for dinner. They can be...a lot."

Michel squeezed his hand before gently interrupting him. "Brett. I don't want to talk about your sisters either. Not when we're here, alone, on this gorgeous, secluded island. I'd much rather talk about kissing every inch of your body tonight."

Brett spluttered even though he wasn't eating or drinking anything. *Breathe, dammit.*

Michel chuckled, clearly misinterpreting Brett's reaction. "We'll deal with your family together. There's no reason to worry about them right here and now."

Brett wasn't so sure. He picked up his wine glass to take a drink, nodding. Wine with dinner was something he allowed himself. "Of course, yes, no reason to worry about them. But... tomorrow, what do you think about going on a romantic hike? Get away from the hotel and the other guests for a while?"

"Is hiking romantic?" Michel asked, his heated gaze replaced with a frown.

Brett laughed. The man had a point. But their best recourse was to avoid Patience and Evelyn and their activity options outside the resort were limited. Apart from the small airstrip and the resort, the island was uninhabited. The staff of the resort must live somewhere nearby, but everything was flown in, from food to building supplies. Further proof that private islands were an outrageous and impractical expense. Their choices were sailing or hiking, and he knew Michel held a deep-seated dislike of boats and all boat-related things.

"It is when you're on a private island," Brett said, giving Michel a saucy grin.

Michel's frown cleared and he smirked. "I mean, if you're there, I suppose anything could be romantic."

Brett raised his eyebrows. "Wow... That may actually have been the cheesiest thing anyone's ever said to me."

Michel nodded. "By which you mean the most romantic."

"Do I?"

The look Michel gave him could only be described as smoldering. His eyelids were lowered, his mouth unsmiling, lips slightly parted, his chest rising and falling. Then, his eyes fixed on Brett's, he bit his lower lip.

Brett let out a noise that sounded a lot like a whimper. He broke eye contact, cleared his throat, and looked back down at his plate. His jeans were uncomfortably tight and he found breathing to be a challenge in a way it hadn't been a moment ago. Was Michel about to throw the table over, leap into his lap, devour his mouth, and tear his clothes off? Did he want him to? He did, but he also didn't know what he'd do if it happened. Would he be able to give in to the moment, or would he freak out about what happened when the moment ended? Was there really some fear in him that Michel would be over Brett once they'd had sex? Or that Brett would be so bad in bed Michel would break up with him and avoid him? Even voicing them in his head, the worries sounded ridiculous, but they were there and were clearly fucking with him. "All right, all right, we know there's a reason you've been voted sexiest man alive five times. You don't need to demonstrate it."

Shit, now he sounded pissed off about Michel being sexy. Michel should dump him immediately. He was obviously not boyfriend material, as his ex-girlfriends would be happy to attest to.

He drained the rest of his wine glass, something he hadn't done in a while. Usually, he was good about sipping alcohol instead of inhaling it. But that was when he wasn't about to come out of his skin, when the steak he was devouring didn't suddenly stick to his throat, when he was trying to navigate this boundary between friendship and boyfriendship and failing at it.

When he set the empty glass down, he found Michel watching him, one hand loosely wrapped around his fork, the other casually resting on the table.

"What?" Brett asked, trying desperately to push away his unbearable self-consciousness.

Michel looked like he wanted to say something but then didn't. His frown returned as he asked, "Where are we hiking tomorrow?"

"Oh, um, I stopped by the front desk on the way back up here and they gave me a map of the hiking trips around here. We'll leave early in the morning."

At the early-in-the-morning part, Michel's frown deepened. "Early in the morning? How early?"

"Seven?"

Michel groaned. Even though the groan was in displeasure, the sound was erotic, just like every sound Michel made, and Brett was right back where he was—on edge and wondering if he should jump.

He didn't jump. He cleared his throat and returned the banter.. "Don't you have insanely early calls when you're on set? Like 5:00 am?"

"Not voluntarily. I don't know who gets up at that hour of their own accord," Michel grumbled as he cut off a piece of his steak.

Brett laughed. "People who are trying to avoid running into other people."

Michel sighed. "Fine, but you'd better be bringing coffee. And if I'm too tired, you have to carry me."

"You know I have almost zero muscles, right? Unlike you, I might add," Brett said, taking the moment to ogle said muscles. It wasn't the first time Brett had wondered how Michel maintained his physique. Usually, someone so well-toned spent quality time at the gym on a daily basis. Michel exercised, but he was generally too busy to work out. It was one of the great unsolved mysteries of Michel Polce. Magazines had devoted whole issues to speculation on the subject.

Michel spent the rest of the meal coming up with worst-case scenarios for their hiking adventure while Brett refuted them or explained in exaggerated detail how he'd get them out of the situation. It was just like when they were friends, before Michel had started dating Sylvia and moved to the house in the hills. Before there was anything romantic between them, merely the tension of a something that neither of them could put words to. Brett finally relaxed.

After he'd set their dishes outside the door and they'd moved into the sitting area, Brett found out what Michel had avoided saying earlier.

Michel lounged on the teal couch, toying with a glass of whiskey, one leg crossed over the other, leaning into the cushions. Brett took a seat near him but not so near that they were touching. It was the game of who would cross the line from conversation to kissing. Who would make the first move?

As Brett drank a glass of water, trying to keep his nerves at bay, Michel changed the rules of the game.

"We can be honest with each other, can't we, Brett?" Michel asked, his voice low and soft.

Brett froze, then slowly lowered his glass back to the coaster. He had no idea where this was going. It wasn't like he told Michel everything, he couldn't. He'd never told Michel about his heavy drinking days—he was too ashamed of the person he'd been. And there were secrets Lucille had told him while they were dating. Delicious, scandalous secrets he'd heard only after swearing never to repeat them on pain of death. He didn't think Michel was talking about these things, and yet he froze like he had a guilty conscience. "Yes," he said, his voice so soft it was almost inaudible. He couldn't look at Michel.

Michel heard him because he responded. "That's what I'd like, too. So, will you please tell me what's going on with you?"

Brett turned his head quickly and met Michel's worried gaze. "What are you talking about?"

Michel sighed, but it didn't sound exasperated, it sounded more, sad? "We rushed into things. There was the not-party and the crime club, and then you went back to the city and I went home. We've been busy living our own lives, talking, yes, but essentially going back to where we were before. I was hoping this weekend we could actually move forward into this relationship of ours. After today, I'm not sure it would be best for you."

Brett didn't know what to say. He opened his mouth and then, when nothing came out, Michel spoke again.

"If you feel this was all too much too fast or you realized you got caught up in something you don't actually feel, I'll understand. We can go back to being friends, if that's what you want. Or you can have nothing to do with me, whatever you need."

Brett closed his mouth. His mind reeled. He wanted to shout that he was nervous and felt like a teenager, scared shitless that the person he *liked* liked him back. He wanted to reassure Michel he had the hots for him, that he had for a longer than he knew. He wanted to confess all his fears, his secrets, his desires. He wanted to tell Michel he liked...no, *loved* him and probably would always love him, but he had so many self-esteem and anxiety issues that he couldn't shake the fear Michel would tire of him and leave. He wanted to tell Michel everything.

But he couldn't say all those things. He didn't know where to begin. What he needed to do, more than anything, was show him that he didn't want to break up, didn't want to slow down. And he needed to do something soon before the silence became his answer. In a move that shouldn't have worked given his general lack of coordination, Brett launched himself across the couch, landing in Michel's lap and squirming until he had one leg on either side of his hips, his hands on his face, his eyes intent on Michel's, their lips inches apart.

"I want you, Michel. I've wanted you for longer than I know," he said, barely able to get the words out as his heart thudded, blood rushed in his ears, and he fought the desire to press his body even closer. He had to know that Michel didn't want to get out, didn't want to go back to friends. Had to have that confirmation that it was okay to kiss him and go further than kissing him. "Is this what you want?"

Michel's look of surprise when Brett leaped into his lap turned into heat, a return of the seductive smolder he'd shown off at dinner. He nodded.

Brett didn't stop, didn't let his emotions choke him, didn't overthink what he was doing. He closed the small gap and claimed Michel's mouth.

If someone had told Brett a year ago kissing Michel was going to become his new favorite activity, he would have considered the idea and then dismissed it as improbable. Granted, at the time, he and Michel were barely speaking and Brett was trying to drown his failure and family dysfunction in a whiskey bottle like some sort of artist cliché. The idea he would even be speaking to Michel in a year's time would have seemed ridiculous to that version of Brett.

Fortunately, that version had been replaced with the Brett whose tongue was now tracing Michel's lower lip. He slid his hands back into Michel's hair, his beautiful, dark, still damp hair, his back arching as he pressed his body closer. Michel helped by gripping Brett's hips and pulling him in, holding tight until they both groaned.

Michel's mouth opened as he deepened the kiss. They were devouring each other's faces, and it was the single hottest moment of Brett's life.

The casual thought that if things got hotter every time he kissed Michel he'd someday spontaneously combust floated through his brain. If that were the way he'd go, what a way it would be.

Michel's fingers, his devilishly skilled fingers that wrote wicked lines one moment and played a heart-wrenching sonata the next, inched up Brett's sides, fiddling with the hem of his t-shirt.

Brett broke away, desperately needing to catch his breath but also to pull off the damn shirt. Michel's head fell back, his eyes bright and burning as he watched Brett. Then Brett's hands were on the buttons of Michel's shirt and he was desperately trying not to destroy Michel's awfully expensive wardrobe while also getting skin-to-skin as fast as possible. He didn't know where this boldness was coming from, what dam had broken inside him to overpower his inhibitions. It was something he could circle back to later. Right now, he had a shirt to tackle.

"Michel," Brett said in between quick, smacking kisses. "You have to start wearing things without buttons."

Michel, whose roaming hands were making the unbuttoning even harder, laughed. "I'll keep that in mind."

"I don't suppose I could just rip it off?"

The desire in Michel's face flickered out, his hands stilling against Brett's burning skin. "Well…"

Brett broke into a smile and kissed Michel's stunned mouth. "I would never."

"Such a tease, Brett," Michel said, matching Brett's smile and getting back into gear.

"No, this"—Brett gestured to the area where their erections were straining to get to each other, hampered by far too much fabric and zippers— "is a tease. We need to get naked. Like now."

Michel's hands were on Brett's jeans before he could finish that sentence. "Couldn't agree more."

Brett was about to dive back in on the buttons, when his phone buzzed. He turned to look at it where it lay on the table behind him. It buzzed again.

"I should turn that off. It's probably just Lucille texting to complain about us being gone and her having no one to hang out with." Which would be true under different circumstances but not in this case. If it was Lucille, she wasn't texting a life update. She'd be texting to complain about Noah and his latest horrible idea. Right then, Brett didn't care two fucks about Noah.

"Hurry," Michel said, his voice sounding desperate in a way Brett loved.

Brett stood and moved over to pick up his phone. Before looking at it, he glanced at Michel. Michel, who was splayed on that couch, his clothing mussed, his hair a mess, his breathing heavy, and arousal radiating off of him. Brett had never seen anything as beautiful, and it took his breath away to know Michel was like this because of things they had done.

Then he looked down at the phone and blinked. It was Lucille, but what she'd written didn't make sense. Her first text read, *Guess who our next client is?* Followed by, *Sylvia. That's who.*

A knock at the door.

Brett, trying to figure out what Lucille could be telling him, walked to the door on autopilot. He turned the handle, pulled it open, and looked up into the impatient face of his sister Evelyn. *Fuck.*

The mood was, unquestionably, ruined.

Chapter Nine

Lucille skipped the film screening. She never attended screenings or concerts, preferring to concentrate on her client's unscripted public moments. Leave the other events to the PR specialists. They could handle the red carpet and the press interviews. Lucille would show up where she was most needed—at the after-party.

It took most of the day for her to get over her anger with Simon and Noah, catch up on her endless barrage of messages, and prepare for the evening ahead. Her client was the film's director. Normally, she didn't work with directors. They weren't as easily recognized as the actors and therefore didn't appear in the types of publications she leaked stories to. This director was different. He had a terrible habit of accepting bribes from up-and-coming actors in front of at least half a dozen media personal and industry rivals. During their first meeting, he'd explained at length how he only accepted monetary bribes and everyone did it so why should he be persecuted? Lucille, with great effort, held her tongue and agreed to spin the scandal for him. Provided he started using more caution and did what everyone else did, which was to accept the money in private.

Someday, she might get to be more selective in her choice of clients again. Someday when the business had fully recovered from her departure and Simon's reputation. Not today.

She timed her arrival at the club to coincide with a sizable influx of guests. The media and paparazzi, distracted by big-name attendees, didn't notice her slip through the door. The color of the season was blush, and so she wore blush, effectively blending in with the crowd. Those who wanted to stand out wore daring colors, those who wanted to be on trend wore the trend. Lucille didn't ever want to stand out, but if she ever met this year's trendsetter, she was going to have some harsh words about the color blush.

The party took over the entire club. The entrance led into a large reception area, lit in soft blues and purples and decorated in white and, of course, blush. Couches and armchairs were clustered together to create intimate seating along the walls.

Servers passed trays of appetizers and glasses of champagne. The mood on this level was seductive, charming, relaxing. Cocktail tables dotted the center of the space, and Lucille was not at all happy to discover her dress matched the table linens.

As she strolled around the room, sipping on soda water, she cataloged those present. A couple of current clients, a few celebrities she personally thought could use her services, and a lot of people she didn't know in the slightest. An unsurprising gathering.

She reached a glittering white staircase and descended to the dance floor below. On this level, the vibe changed. Many of the guests were dancing, others grouped around the bar, laughing and staking their claim on the easy access to drinks. A DJ played techno remixes of pop songs and the celebrities put on a show of having a great time.

Her client wasn't hard to spot. He stood at the center of one of the bar side clusters, talking out of his ass, the group hanging on his every word. As she watched from her inconspicuous spot against the wall, he literally accepted a check from one of the men in the group, looked at it, folded it, and grinned. He slapped the guy on the back and told him, loudly, to report to the studio on Monday. The whole interaction was filmed by another member of the group who, like just about everyone, knew how to take a video on a smartphone.

Whether it was her still smoldering anger with Simon and Noah and their terrible decisions or that she was experiencing a change of heart about representing misogynistic dicks, she was done. Her brain chatted away at her, telling her all the ways she could spin the video into a crowd-pleasing, humanitarian act of goodwill, but dammit, she didn't want to. She fumed. The guy hadn't listened to one word she said. One moment, he said he'd be more discreet and the next, he was standing in the middle of a crowd at the premiere party for his movie, accepting money in full view of a hundred witnesses, in direct contradiction to everything she told him. Sure, she could spin it. She'd gotten celebrities out of stickier situations. But this one, for whatever reason, she didn't give a shit about.

Lucille kept her body language calm and relaxed as she ascended the staircase and made for the door. Before she could make her escape, a hand grabbed her arm and pulled her into one of the dimly lit corners. "What the fuck?" she said, ready to land a punch on whoever dared to manhandle her. When she saw it was Noah, her desire to commit body harm didn't decrease one bit.

"Noah. What the hell are you doing here?" she hissed at him.

Yes, she noticed he looked amazing in his black, glittering tuxedo. Lucille had only seen one other man who could rock a tux the way Noah rocked his and that man was currently on an island with her ex-boyfriend.

Yet, unlike Michel's show-stopping ensembles, Noah looked exactly as a spin doctor should, stylish yet utterly forgettable. At least to anyone who wasn't her.

All of this she noted without breaking her glare. The last thing she needed was for him to think she found him attractive.

Noah glanced around at the other guests. "Not here. We need somewhere private. Does this place have some sort of super-secluded alcove?"

Lucille didn't need to check out the space around her to know a room full of celebrities, even a loud party where everyone was drunk, was never the place to talk. And the indignant yelling she planned to do would not only be observed, it would be remarked on, photographed, and possibly filmed if she were particularly unlucky. So, instead of the snarky retort she wanted to make, she said, "Not that I know of. I doubt I've been here much longer than you have."

Noah, still checking out the area, said, "We can't leave. There has to be somewhere..."

Suddenly, he grabbed her hand and said, "Come on."

Lucille wrenched her hand from his grasp like she didn't want to get burned because *let's face it. I don't want to get burned.* "I'm perfectly capable of walking on my own."

His head turned in her direction, but he didn't say anything. He led the way through the crowd, gracefully avoiding the groups of chatting and drinking gaiety. At one point, a young woman who Lucille thought looked vaguely familiar in a grown-up child star sort of way, tripped and went crashing into Noah as he passed. He caught the woman, righted her, and gave her a panty-dropping grin. She smiled back at him and he told her something before continuing on his way.

Lucille took a wide arc around the teetering starlet, feeling sulky. Something about Noah's little rescue rubbed her all wrong. Was she jealous of his charm? She could be charming when she needed to be, but it was a widely accepted fact between the two of them that Simon charmed and Lucille strong-armed. Simon distracted and diverted, Lucille told outright lies. And Noah...Noah made people feel like he'd go to the ends of the earth to help them and it would be his absolute pleasure. Even if the assistance was only righting a toppling party-goer.

He stopped at the opposite side of the club. In front of him was a leather couch, pushed up against the corner. Hazy drapes, lit with a soft purple glow, half hid the couch from the rest of the room. It wasn't a secluded alcove or a private room but, given the options available, she begrudgingly agreed it would have to do. This was, of course, going off the assumption Noah was right and they couldn't leave the party yet. After all, she might not have done what she'd come to do, but she'd done all she planned to.

"After you," he said, extending his arm to offer her a seat.

Yeah right. Like I'm going to be trapped against the wall while he has free rein to get up and leave when he wants. "Absolutely not. You sit first," she replied with fake sweetness.

Noah sat. Lucille took a seat across from him in a white faux leather armchair.

"Lucille," Noah said, giving her a nonplussed look and drawing her name out.

She raised her eyebrows and waited for him to say more, but he didn't. She crossed her right leg over her left, knowing it hiked her dress up.

She wasn't disappointed. He glanced down at her leg and then blinked and fixed his gaze firmly on her face, his brown eyes unreadable.

"Are you trying to seduce me, Ms. Anton?" he asked in a deep, dramatic tone.

Lucille was caught off guard. Her surprise lasted only long enough for her to raise her eyebrows. She thought about how to react, running through the possibilities swiftly. She reminded herself of her earlier resolution to let him screw up his life all on his own. Her resolution that she couldn't be angry with him because she didn't care enough to be. And yet... "You wish," she said, taking another sip of her soda water.

He seemed like he was about to say, "I do wish," but then looked away and changed the subject.

Interesting.

"Lucille...Simon told me about what happened." His voice lost all of its usual smooth edge.

Lucille didn't need to ask what Simon had told him about. She knew it was the night at Michel's, the night Sylvia held her, Brett, and Michel at gunpoint, nearly killing them.

"I honestly didn't know," he said, his face contrite like he was feeling her pain, empathizing with what she'd gone through. It was a powerful move, one she could almost believe was genuine.

Lucille scoffed. She'd had time to think about why she was so upset about them working with Sylvia. Time to sort through the feelings and find what was at the ugly heart of her anger. It had nothing to do with Sylvia's attempt on their life. Sure, Sylvia had threatened her two best friends, and that pissed her off a lot. But Simon was absolutely right about all the reasons they should take her on as a client. Sylvia Stanton was a gold mine, especially if the rumors were true and she'd patched things up with her father. She was America's favorite heiress, a consummate partier, fashion icon, social media influencer, and she had a terrible temper. She was the next best thing to having Michel Polce as a client, and since they already had the one, why not make it a set? The rare trading cards of celebrity spin doctoring.

"Yeah, I got that," she said, her voice clipped and cold.

"Okay, so why are you mad at me? Do you not want us to work with her?" Noah asked, frowning, his questions trying to burrow into her, to get to her secrets.

Lucille itched to reach over and smooth those frown lines, to take away his confusion. It irritated her how much she wanted to tell him things, how much she wanted to touch him, how she couldn't stop thinking about their kisses and wanting more of that heat, the potent combination of dislike and attraction fueling their passion. Her next words came out harsher than she'd intended. "You work for both Simon and me, remember? If you're taking on a celebrity as a client, that's my side of the business, as you well know. If this is going to work, I need final say on your clients."

She didn't know how she expected him to react. She didn't know how she should react. It was one of the first completely honest speeches she'd ever given. It was vulnerable putting her needs out on the table. If Noah decided to fight her on this, she was going to drop some more truth bombs and tell him exactly what she thought of his methods of sneaking around and stealing flash drives.

But instead of armoring up, Noah did something completely unexpected. He gave a slight shiver, so quick she almost didn't catch it, and for a moment, his eyes blazed with want. A second later, it was gone, his face an expressionless mask again. "Fine," he said. "Then you should know I have a meeting with her tomorrow."

Lucille was stuck on the brief response she'd observed. She wasn't usually so serious and direct, hell, she avoided open honesty if at all possible, but Noah's reaction was intriguing. He'd also enjoyed being pressed against the side of the building the night before and when they'd first kissed at the charity event. She didn't know what she'd do with this information yet, but she certainly had some ideas. Unfortunately, they all involved breaking her vow not to spend any more time around him than she had to.

"And I do need your help," Noah added, doing that thing where he stared at her with bold openness.

Lucille pretended her heart wasn't beating faster and the heat she felt was the aftermath of her rage. Outwardly, she smirked. "Why don't we ditch this party and go somewhere we can talk freely? Then you can try to convince me to help you."

Noah shook his head. "Well..."

"You didn't just come here to apologize," Lucille guessed.

"No," he said slowly.

"What does Simon want me to do now?"

He leaned forward, putting his hands on his knees and getting closer to her.

Lucille uncrossed her legs and leaned into him so he could deliver his message. She did not think about them being close enough to kiss.

"Simon's trying to get one of the executive producers on this movie to work with him. Apparently, the guy's a scandal magnet. He's been married four times, has been involved in multiple Ponzi schemes, and is one bad press release from getting sued for all he's worth."

"Oh, good Lord," Lucille said, leaning back. She could easily follow Simon's line of thinking. If the producer thought Simon could keep his name out of future scandals and keep him out of jail, it would be a huge account. "Has he reached out at all?"

Noah shook his head. "He thought it would be better received coming from you."

She narrowed her eyes. *Lovely.* She knew what they meant. The guy was more likely to be intrigued by a beautiful woman than a man in a sparkly tux.

"You don't have to do it if you don't want to," he added.

Lucille set her drink down. "Point him out to me and then disappear. Don't let him see you in case you end up working with him later. Where is he?"

He casually scanned the area.

Lucille kept her gaze on him.

"He's on the move at your four. Heading toward the door."

"Watch and learn."

CHAPTER TEN

Lucille didn't check to see if Noah was watching her and hoped he was. It thrilled her to have an audience to show off to. A rare occurrence indeed.

The process of engaging a client typically went one of two ways. The first was the method Lucille had used with Michel. One of her current clients had let slip that a celebrity wanted to meet her, and she arranged to bump into him at a premiere and talk business. Word of mouth had gained her most of her clients and lost Simon most of his after he returned from his exile. A terribly effective method wherein a client's acquaintance sees how well said client is doing with their reputation and media image. The client discreetly offers to introduce the acquaintance to their secret weapon. Lucille or Simon meets the person and decides whether to work with them. One of the first rules Simon taught her about celebrity spin doctoring had been to always meet a new client at an event. For one thing, he said, there would be drinks, and for another, the best cover, especially when working with celebrities, was a crowd of equally famous people.

Their other method was the one Lucille was currently engaged in. Simon identified someone he wanted to work with and she was going to make the initial introductions. She'd approach the mark, either indirectly by hanging out at a table nearby and jumping in at the right moment in a conversation or, as she had to do now, directly out of timely necessity. She'd bump into him, apologize, and then recognize him. Then suggest he give her company a call, that they could do a lot for him. She'd slip him a card, press it into his hand, and then get the hell out before he got any ideas about her meaning more than she said.

That part at least went according to plan. Lucille slipped through the crowd, clearing a path by walking purposefully and looking like someone for whom paths were cleared. She executed the collision just as the producer neared the door.

"Oh, my God, I'm so sorry," she said, placing a hand on his arm as though to steady herself.

The producer, a man by the name of George Lampart, took in her hand on his arm and her appearance with small blue eyes. Then he laughed and smiled with teeth that were too white. He winked at her. "Well, that's okay, little lady," he said with a deep boom of a voice.

Lucille tried not to wonder what his four ex-wives saw in him. She couldn't stand a man who winked. She released his arm and feigned recognition. "Wait a minute, aren't you...no, you couldn't be..."

"Couldn't be who, darlin'?" he asked.

Lucille resisted the urge to knee him in the balls. After all, she didn't even want to work with the guy. She continued. "You're George Lampart, the executive producer," she exclaimed and gave him a sly, knowing smile.

The producer agreed he was who she said he was.

Lucille pulled her card out of her tiny evening purse. "I'm so glad we ran into each other—"

"Now, don't tell me you're an actress looking for your big break. Because I'm very picky about who I recommend for my films," he said in a tone that clearly suggested he'd be willing to bend the rules if she slept with him.

She laughed. "Oh, no, you misunderstand, Mr. Lampart. I think my business partner and I can help you. We know all about those things you've done." Here, she raised her eyebrows to show she wasn't going to say what the things were in public but he should assume she knew the worst of the worst. "And we can make sure no one else knows. Ever."

"What are you—" He frowned.

"Think on it." She pressed the card into his hand. Then she sauntered away, relieved to be out of his vicinity. She went to where Noah stood against the wall, looking casually inconspicuous. She swept past him.

He caught the hint and followed her.

"And that's how it's done," she said quietly in his direction.

She thought she heard him say, "Impressive," but couldn't be sure.

Everything continued to go to plan until they left the building and found their potential new client pressed against a car, his wrists in handcuffs, held in place by a police officer reading him his rights.

"Fuck," Lucille said because there wasn't anything else to say. She said it again when she saw who stood beside the police officer.

Lucille hadn't seen Detective Matt Adams since their conversation in his office when she'd made it clear they were never getting back together. She'd hoped to keep it that way. And yet, here they were again, going after the same target. She had to stop working with people who were wanted by the police. *Although,* she reminded herself, *this one is all Simon's doing.*

Lucille had paused when she saw George Lampart being arrested and froze when she saw Matt standing by the car, frowning at the producer. Noah bumped into her and stayed close, so close she could feel the heat of his body in the night air.

"Well, that sucks," Noah said. "Not much we can do, though. Shall we get out of here?"

His pause between each statement was presumably because of Lucille's lack of reaction. When he asked if they should leave, she nodded, her brain urging her to get out before Matt noticed them.

But today wasn't her day and tonight vowed to get worse, so of course, the moment Lucille started to back away, Matt looked up and locked eyes with her.

Matt Adams had always been gorgeous in a muscular, law-abiding way. He'd been Lucille's boyfriend when she'd first moved in with Simon permanently, when she was still a teenager without a purpose who thought platform flip-flops were chic. They weren't great together. She kept her burgeoning spin doctor career from Matt, and he kept trying to mold her into the perfect police officer's girlfriend. Then there was the business with him arresting Simon and Lucille had never forgiven him. Especially when she discovered Matt had been keeping tabs on her for eight years because he hadn't moved on. And then he shot her in the shoulder.

His face morphed from surprise to confusion to hurt and finally landed on failed steely indifference. "Lucy," he breathed, the tone of his voice further negating his attempt at stoicism.

"Hello, Matt," Lucille said in perfect, calm detachment. She was practiced at emotional control, after all, and whatever she may be feeling internally, it didn't show unless she wanted it to.

"What are you doing here?" he asked, his voice sharp now. His gaze flicked briefly over her shoulder to where Noah stood.

Lucille was preparing her icy reply when Noah jumped in. First, he moved so he stood beside her. "Well, Detective," he said, his voice holding a trace of amusement. "I presume since you two seem to be old friends, you're familiar with Lucille's work?"

It was a little thing, but the fact Noah had called her Lucille, especially after Matt had used her childhood nickname as though he had a right to, warmed her. She normally couldn't stand men answering questions she was asked but found she wanted to hear where Noah was going with this.

Matt nodded, his eyes narrowing in suspicion. He stepped closer to them, his back to the curious police officer who'd finished telling Mr. Lampart his rights and hauled him into the squad car.

"I thought as much. We were considering working with Mr. Lampart over there. But since you've got him under control, we'll take our leave. Can't go impeding the process of the law now, can we?" Noah probably accompanied the speech with a grin. Lucille didn't look at him to check. She watched Matt, her eyes narrowed.

Matt frowned deeper. He seemed to be deciding what to say. Perhaps deciding whether to demand to know who this impertinent stranger was or to ask why Lucille was once again soliciting business from known criminals. In the end, he must have landed on his usual route of condescending judgment. "I thought you'd stopped doing this kind of shit, Lucy."

Lucille gritted her teeth. She wanted to punch him. "I thought we'd decided you have absolutely no say in what I do."

Matt sighed, running his hand through his hair like he used to do when they were dating. Now, his hair had more streaks of gray in it, a look that made him more distinguished in a thoroughly irritating way. "I worry about you. That's all."

Lucille was hyperaware of Noah beside her and wished he wasn't there to witness this. She found, when third-party observers saw her interactions with Matt, they tended to side with him. He came across as lovelorn and heartbroken while Lucille acted like a heartless bitch. It wasn't like she could explain their long history, their complete incompatibility, or the fact Matt had shot her in the shoulder. Not without getting others in trouble.

She tried to tell herself she didn't care what Noah thought of her. He probably already considered her a heartless bitch. What did it matter if he was given some more proof?

Somehow, though, it mattered.

"You have no right," she said, her voice low and as dangerous as she could make it.

"Really?" Matt said, crossing his arms. "And when you finally run out of luck and end up on my wanted list, who do you expect to save you then?"

Noah broke in again. "Your wanted list? What are you, a bounty hunter?"

Lucille glanced at him.

Noah had his arms folded and a smirk on his face.

Matt shifted his whole body along with his attention, so it was very obvious to everyone he was now talking to Noah. "I hope you aren't planning to get involved with her. She'll use you and throw you away without a moment's hesitation. She's not capable of loving anyone but herself."

With the way he said it, deep and venomous, he meant it to hurt.

Lucille felt a tiny twinge in the region of her heart that clung on to things like old relationships and forgotten loves. But that was all. She wondered when she'd started to hate Matt. Certainly, there was no danger of love lost between them. But when had she begun to loathe him? It didn't matter. Not anymore.

"That is—" Noah started.

But Lucille didn't want him to defend her.

She let out a deep, condescending sigh. "Oh, Matt. No. That's beneath you."

His face flushed and he opened his mouth to speak, but she shook her head. She leaned in until she was close enough to whisper in his ear. "Get over yourself and move on. Because if you don't? I'll destroy you. Stay the fuck away from me."

She backed up and gave him her most dangerous smile. "Glad we got that cleared up." She turned and strolled down the street.

If Matt replied, she was too far away to hear and too over it to listen. Lucille spotted her car as she turned the corner. She slid in, Noah behind her, and directed the driver to take her to her house. Then she leaned back against the leather seats and looked at him.

"What?" she asked.

"Impressive," he said softly, echoing his earlier compliment.

She looked away but knew she wasn't successful at hiding her smile.

They didn't talk the rest of the way to her place. Lucille sensed the tension in the silence but, for once, she didn't know how to break it. She wanted to ask him about the moment in the club where she'd snapped at him and his heated reaction. She'd wanted to ask him since it happened.

It wasn't until they were inside her apartment that she realized she didn't know where Noah was staying or why he'd followed her home. It had seemed natural for him to leave with her, natural for them to return to the same place.

"I can't believe you dated a cop," he said, tugging on his bow tie until it came undone.

Lucille continued her trajectory to the kitchen. "How do you know I dated him?"

The sound of his footsteps followed her as she entered the large space. She went directly to a cupboard and retrieved two glasses and a bottle of bourbon.

When he didn't respond, she turned to him. He sat at the white marble-topped island, giving her a look that clearly communicated how much he didn't enjoy being considered stupid.

"Please," he said. "The guy radiated heartbreak and hurt feelings."

She nodded. "I know. It's basically his aftershave."

She poured out two rather full glasses of bourbon, added a large ice cube to each, and slid one across the island to him.

"Thanks," he said, catching the drink. "So. What's the story with you two? Things didn't work out?"

Lucille studied Noah. A piece of black hair fell across his forehead, and it was the only part of his appearance at all out of place. He met her gaze with dark-brown eyes, watching her even as he lifted the glass to his lips and took a drink. She was reminded of her reaction when they first met. The excitement of attraction and lust that led to them making out. Twice. But there was something else there after this weird outing together. Something akin to not loathing him entirely.

Was that all it took? A guy only had to stand up to her ex-boyfriend and she was all ready to start liking him? But it wasn't that he'd stood up to Matt. After all, she could take care of herself, she didn't need any help there. And yet...something had changed.

It wasn't like she wanted to marry the guy. She just maybe wasn't going to hate him as much.

Lucille smiled and took a sip of her brandy. It slid down her throat, warming instead of burning. It was the good stuff. "He's the one who arrested Simon and had him falsely accused of murder."

Noah blew out his breath forcefully. "And he thought you'd still want to be with him after that? I took on one client without asking you, and I'm lucky you're still talking to me."

"You are." She smiled because she wanted to.

"I know," he replied.

They were both silent for a moment, drinking and not looking at each other. She decided to add the other part. "And then he shot me in the shoulder during the whole Sylvia incident."

She both did and did not get the reaction she was expecting. First, he said, "And, again, he still thought you'd want to get back together with him?"

Then he slowly dragged his gaze away from hers, down her face and neck, to her shoulder.

Lucille shivered and hoped he didn't notice. It was a good move. Wrong shoulder, but good move.

"Mm," she said, looking away and blinking hard. "Whatever you do, don't date a cop."

"How do you feel about former private investigators?"

Her eyes shot back to his face. His expression was guarded. She couldn't tell if he was serious or not. He couldn't be serious. He had to know there was no way they could date. For one thing, she'd only just decided she didn't completely despise him—she wasn't about to jump into a relationship with him. For another, he lived in a different city, hours away from her. How would that even work?

Her mind offered a couple of solutions to the long-distance thing, which she dismissed.

Instead, she threw in a Simon Anton spin doctor tactic. She changed the subject to something he had to engage on. "Don't you have a flight to catch or something?"

"Didn't I tell you? My meeting with Sylvia is in LA."

"Fine, then a hotel?"

Noah raised an eyebrow at her. "How am I supposed to convince you to go to the meeting with me if I'm at a hotel?"

"I don't know. Text me?" Lucille offered.

He narrowed his eyes at her.

She narrowed hers back at him.

They stared at each other, silently.

She broke first, her voice firm. "Fine. You can stay here for one night. You'll be in the guest room, and we'll talk about the meeting tomorrow. It's late, and I'm going to bed."

Noah, not breaking eye contact, said, with undeniable heat in his voice, "You're the boss."

CHAPTER ELEVEN

B rett resisted his initial impulse to slam the door in Evelyn's face. He did close it more, using his body to block her view of the room and hoping against hope she hadn't seen Michel. "Evie," he croaked, "what're you doing here?"

Evelyn smirked at him. She'd changed out of her Michel photo dress into a sequined tank top and cutoffs, which surprisingly, did not have anything about Michel on them. Unless, Brett realized with a sinking certainty, she was wearing one of those sequins shirts that revealed something when the sequins were pushed up. Like Michel's face. "I lost the bet. Patience cheated, of course, but she won't admit it. Are you going to act like a total weirdo all night or are you coming?"

He blinked at her. "Coming where?"

"Drinks? In the bar? We talked about this?"

Brett could have sworn this was the first time he'd heard about these plans. But he didn't want to seem suspicious by refusing. "Right. Give me five minutes to change. I'll meet you down there."

As soon as Evelyn was gone, he closed the door and turned to face Michel. "So, that was my sister."

Michel had buttoned his shirt and straightened his hair. "I gathered."

Their splintered moment hung in the air, intrusive and unspoken. "I have to go have drinks with them or they'll come back."

"Yes."

"I'll be back as soon as I can." Brett couldn't seem to stop talking. He thought Michel seemed upset. How could he not be when they'd been interrupted by his siblings twice in one day? "I wish you could come with me but... it's better this way. They are kind of horrible and—"

"Brett. I get it. Just go."

Dismissed, he changed and left. Before he could collect his thoughts, let alone his emotions, he was in the hotel bar facing his sisters. They sat close to each other at a circular booth, leaving the other end open for him to slide in. Patience wore an over-size poncho in gray and black leggings, in defiance of the tropical heat. She had her green glasses on and looked like she was about to write something scathing about anyone who dared talk to her.

"Hope we weren't interrupting anything," Evelyn said, raising her eyebrows meaningfully.

Brett shook his head. "No, no, not at all," he said with a forced smile. Evelyn wasn't someone to keep things to herself. If she'd seen Michel, she'd have said so. He didn't care what she thought she saw, as long as it wasn't him.

"Really? Because you came down here awfully quickly," said Patience with a frown. "Almost like you didn't want us to come back up to your room. Like you don't want us to meet this friend of yours?"

"Coworker," Brett replied, trying desperately to find a way to change the topic.

The server passed by their table. His sisters ordered fresh cocktails. Brett ordered a soda water with lemon.

He felt a momentary pang for the relief alcohol would provide him. But being drunk around these two was the single worst thing he could do. Drunk Brett told secrets, confessed truths, and waxed poetic about his latest obsession. All three of which would inevitably lead to Michel.

When the server left, he opened his mouth to ask Patience about her work. But she beat him to the punch.

"Coworker? From where?"

Brett blinked in surprise. There was something about Patience's expression, a glint in her eyes that made him wonder for a moment what she knew. "I just told you this afternoon. LT Tech."

"Oh, that's right. It sounded so absurdly dull I immediately forgot about it," she said with a smirk.

Brett relaxed. It was a classic Patience Jacobs move to toy with him, make him believe she had dirt on him. But, he reasoned, even though she thought the fan club business was pointless and trite, she wouldn't hold back from telling Evelyn about Michel's presence. Not when the payoff was bound to be sensationally uncomfortable.

Evelyn rolled her eyes. "Ugh, well, that's no fun. I was hoping you were here with your secret lover or something interesting like that."

Brett frowned. "I'm here with a guy."

"Which would make it all the better," Evelyn said. She huffed. "Instead, it's just the same old boring, straight-laced Brett who doesn't know how to have a good time."

"Hey," Brett protested, totally ignoring for the moment how his sister was okay with him being into guys, not because she was accepting, but for her own added entertainment. "I can be fun. Remember when we went to karaoke? That was fun."

The drinks arrived in the silence that followed this remark.

"That was twelve years ago," said Evelyn. "It's like you've been avoiding us."

Brett looked at Patience. She added her own barb. "He has been avoiding us. Ever since he failed to write his second screenplay."

"Suspicious," Evelyn added.

"I think you're too ashamed to face us," Patience finished in her practical, ego-eviscerating callousness.

Brett gulped at his soda water, wishing again it were stronger and alcoholic. A beverage that could get him out of this conversation would be ideal. He couldn't shake the feeling something was going on. He couldn't see what it was, couldn't get a grasp on the extra component that had been added to their relationship. And he didn't have time to think about it then. They weren't done.

"Definitely ashamed," Evelyn said, "Which makes sense, you know. The rest of us are highly successful. Mom and I have the club and Dad and Patience finish their books."

"And get them published," Patience added.

"Then there's Brett."

They both watched him as they spoke, their eyes intent on his every twitch and shudder. Just as Brett was about to protest that he was actually good at his job and maybe throw in how fucked up it was that their family saw his PhD in biochemistry as a failure, a curious thing happened. Evelyn's gaze flicked away from him. She glanced at something or someone over Brett's shoulder for less than a second, but at this close range, Brett saw it.

He turned his head quickly, trying to see whatever or whoever had caught Evelyn's attention.

The resort bar, even this late into the evening, was crowded with the tanned and tipsy pleasure-seekers who took refuge at The Reef. Refuge from a life of scrutiny and fame, of always being on the precipice of scandal, or at least that was how Brett imagined them to be. He'd been around Michel and the Antons, not to mention his own vulturous family, too long not to know the cost of fame. Here and there, he spotted people he recognized, from parties with Michel or Lucille, from magazine pages, from breaking-news stories. Faces relaxed from hours in the sun, smiling from the loosing effects of their outrageous tropical cocktails, and generally having a great time.

All of this Brett took in in a few seconds, his eyes scanning, trying to figure out what would distract Evelyn. His heart pounded, fearing it was Michel she'd noticed, yet logically knowing it couldn't be. If Evelyn saw Michel in the bar, she wouldn't have looked away so quickly. She'd be all over him before Brett could heroically throw his body in between his sister and his boyfriend.

A glimpse of silvery blonde hair, a long blowout of artificial highlights. Familiar, achingly familiar highlights. He knew that hair.

But it was gone and, however much Brett leaned into the table to try to see more, there was nothing to be seen. He became aware his sisters were still talking about him. Turning back, he found both of them staring at him.

"Decided to join us again?" Evelyn asked.

"Yeah...sorry. Thought I saw someone I knew," Brett said slowly, unable to shake the nagging disappointment of his inability to place the hair.

Evelyn snorted. "I highly doubt there'd be anyone from your circle here at this resort."

Brett again wanted to correct her. He wanted to tell her exactly what circle he ran with now and how it was her who stuck out, not him. But he didn't because the secrets he kept were so much bigger than any of them. And he was powerfully sober.

Patience picked up Evelyn's thread. "It does seem strange you being here. You say your company sent you here on a business trip? Who are you doing business with? What sort of business could a tech company possibly have on a secret resort island for the rich and famous?"

Brett froze and tried to breathe the fruity air, finding it thick and lung-clogging. He needed to channel Lucille. How would she react? What would he say? He took a sip of his soda water to buy himself time. Then he composed his face. Yes, his sisters, by virtue of growing up with him and seeing him at all stages of awkward adolescence, had the unique ability to get through his defenses. But Michel was the most important person in his life, *his person*, and fuck if he wasn't going to protect the man as best he could. "Endorsement deals. We have a new product we're about to unveil and we're on the lookout for the right celebrity to market it."

They didn't look impressed. Patience narrowed her eyes like she was circling him, about to go in for the kill. Evelyn scoffed in open disbelief.

"Why would they send you to get an endorsement deal? As a cautionary tale of how not to screw up your life?" Evelyn asked, derision all over her voice. She was looking away across the room, clearly only half engaged in the conversation, probably hunting for someone to exploit.

The gleam in Patience's eye increased in intensity. "No, Brett's here because he knows the product. He can explain all the boring, technicality shit. Which means your coworker must be someone big, someone to close the deal. You came here, which means you're not looking for the latest media darling rising star. You're looking for a big star. Bring someone big to get someone big."

Brett's body grew cold in the heat of the evening. His heart plummeted through his chest and set up shop somewhere around his stomach. "What are you saying, Patience?" he asked, trying to keep his voice emotionless and hoping he was the only one who caught the high-pitched squeaky quality of it.

"I'm saying this guy you're here with isn't just some coworker. I'm saying it's the CEO of the company, JP Tanaka," Patience said. Her voice was smug, her expression lethal.

At the sound of JP's name, Evelyn snapped her attention back to her sister. "Seriously?"

Brett couldn't speak for the relief. He said a silent apology to JP for what he was about to do and then leaned into the lie. "I'm not telling you who it is."

"Which means I'm right."

Evelyn looked from one of them to the other. "Well, is it JP Tanaka or not?"

"Why do you care?" asked Brett. He knew the answer, Evelyn's motives were not hard to deduce, but he wanted to hear it from her.

"Because he knows Michel, obviously. Honestly, Brett, sometimes you can be such an idiot."

But Brett didn't feel like an idiot. If they thought it was JP he was with, the scrutiny would be off Michel. Although they seemed equally as interested in JP and therefore might try to meet him... *Shit. Why is this so hard?* His conniving siblings were just as intent on his companion as they were when he sat down, more so now they thought it was the billionaire co-CEO of LT Tech.

"I'm not saying if you're right or not," said Brett again. His statement fell on deaf ears.

Evelyn had whipped out her phone and was furiously typing away on the thing. It had a Michel Polce case, of course.

Patience had settled back into the booth, looking smug.

Brett wilted under the full weight of his mistake. Evelyn would want to use JP to get to Michel, to get his phone number or home address or some equally invasive information. Patience would be looking at JP as a career opportunity. A character to investigate, to write about, and to make millions off of with or without his consent. And when they found out it wasn't JP but was really Michel who was Brett's travel companion?

Brett's panic slammed into him, building into a tsunami with lightning speed. He said goodnight to his sisters, who didn't bother saying it back to him. They'd started whispering to each other, scheming most likely.

As he ran back to his room, his fevered brain thought through all the possibilities. They would try to waylay the supposed JP somewhere public, somewhere he couldn't escape without making a scene. Unless they'd taken up kidnapping since he'd last seen them...but no. Brett knew his sisters. Of course, once Evelyn knew it was Michel, all bets were off. The only solution was to get Michel off the island as soon as possible.

He'd have to tell him they were leaving the next day. But how would Michel take the news? It wouldn't just be a hot and heavy moment his sisters ruined, it'd be their whole vacation. No, leaving wouldn't solve anything. Odds were, it'd make their relationship worse. Michel would see how Brett's anxiety ruled his life. How even the threat of a sticky situation had him running.

No, they would stay. If they were out hiking all day and then had dinner in their room again, they could effectively avoid Patience and Evelyn. And tomorrow evening, they'd come up with another plan for the next day. It wasn't perfect, certainly not the way this whole running-away together thing was supposed to work, but it would work.

When Brett finally returned to the room, it was dark. Only the desk lamp cast a small glow in the silence. On the desk was a note. He picked it up, afraid it would be Michel telling him off about earlier. He heard a snore from the bedroom. Michel snored.

The imperfection in his character made Brett smile as he read the note:

Brett,

Since you're dragging me out hiking at the ass crack of dawn, I decided to adhere to an early bedtime. Try not to wake me up.

Michel

There was no *love, Michel* at the end of the note. But it also didn't ask him to sleep on the couch. And Michel hadn't run out on him. In the valley between comfort and unease, Brett called this long first day on the island quits. He slipped into bed next to Michel, cautious to touch him but drawn to his heat. Michel stirred, rolled over, and flopped his body half on top of him. Brett tensed, but Michel didn't wake up. He tried to persuade his body to relax as he listened to the adorable little snuffles and snores his boyfriend made in his sleep. Instead, he stared up at the ceiling, imagining worst-case scenarios. It wasn't until he was finally drifting off to sleep that he remembered the text from Lucille he hadn't responded to. And then, more persistently, the person with the familiar white-blonde hair. Where had he seen that hair before?

Chapter Twelve

Lucille woke early and checked her phone at once. She relaxed when she saw a text from Brett waiting for her. When she hadn't heard back from him after the Sylvia bombshell, she'd been worried. Not about-to-hop-a-plane worried but close. If anything happened to Brett and she could have been there to rescue him but wasn't, she'd never forgive herself. It was still new, this caring-for-people thing. New but not unwelcome. Well, mostly not unwelcome. She wasn't going to begin to deal with her tiny, minuscule, microscopic warm feelings for Noah.

So, Brett's sisters were on the island. Annoying, potentially an issue if they found out about Michel, but not life-threatening. She dashed off a few suggestions and sank back against her pillow, the relief relaxing her tense muscles.

A short while later, she sipped her coffee and scrolled through the search results for Sylvia Stanton. She didn't want to go to this meeting but knew she had to. She didn't care if Sylvia eviscerated Noah, but she sure as hell cared if she destroyed their business. Sylvia knew too much, and it was Lucille's fault she did.

Noah entered the kitchen, yawning and shirtless. Lucille looked up and wished she hadn't. He had a long, muscular, brown torso. No six-pack abs but enough definition to show he worked out. His chest was lightly sprinkled with dark, black hair which led down to the waistband of his sweats.

She realized he was watching her, the sleep gone from his eyes and a wicked little smile on his lips. She looked down at her tablet and tried to focus on something, anything else. "Don't you own a shirt?"

"Actually, I didn't bring any pajamas at all. Found these sweatpants in a drawer in the guest room. I'm guessing they're not Simon's?"

Lucille narrowed her eyes and glanced at the sweatpants, not lingering on how tight they were on Noah, who had substantially more muscles than their owner. When had Brett left sweatpants at her place and why hadn't she found them before?

"Simon wouldn't be caught dead in sweatpants," she said, keeping her voice as deadpan as she could, not meeting his gaze.

Noah had to be loving this. "Well, whoever's they are, I hope he doesn't mind me wearing them."

She didn't respond.

After a moment of silence, he said, "So, what's the breakfast plan?"

She raised her mug of coffee in response. "I don't do breakfast."

"Hm. Mind if I raid your kitchen?"

Lucille didn't care if he ate everything in her house, as long as he put on a damn shirt and stopped talking to her. She picked up her tablet and mug, intending to move to her office where she could strategize in peace. "Fine by me," she said before leaving the room. "I hope you have something to wear for the meeting with Sylvia," she couldn't help adding, combining it with a slow look up and down the half-naked man in her kitchen.

When she returned to his face, she saw a slight flush that betrayed his otherwise impassive response. *Even more interesting.*

"Does this mean you've decided to come with me?" he asked.

"Yes," she said curtly and left.

At the appointed time, Lucille emerged from her office, put on her red power suit, no shirt underneath, and a pair of dangerous-looking black stilettos. She found Noah on his laptop at the kitchen table, dressed in a formfitting black, pinstripe suit, hair styled in an intentionally unruly swoop, and serious concentration replacing the morning flirt. He looked up when she entered, and she thrilled at his momentary speechlessness. Served him right after that shirtless-sweatpants routine.

"Let's get this over with," she said, tossing her dark hair over her shoulder and walking toward the door.

"I feel like it's my turn to ask if you own a shirt," he said.

"It isn't."

The restaurant they were meeting Sylvia at was one Noah picked out. It was off one of the main drags, nestled between a salon and a designer boutique, and it looked like the sort of place that took reservations six months in advance. Lucille approached skeptically. They needed to hide in plain sight and this place looked like the opposite of where they should be. Sylvia Stanton was too easily recognizable and the chances of her making a loud, violent scene when she saw Lucille were high. Inside, however, Lucille found her initial assumption disproven. The interior of the restaurant was segmented into private alcoves and rooms. Instead of wide spaces where diners went to see and be seen, this place was a maze of intrigue and strategically placed potted plants. From where they stood at the host stand, they could hear voices but couldn't see anyone.

Their table was in one of the alcoves, one where the wall curved dramatically, leaving room for only one person to enter at a time. The table was set for three and empty at present.

When the server left, Lucille couldn't help asking, "Where'd you find this place?" After all, she'd never heard of it and she'd been in the city far longer than Noah. She knew all the places for meeting clients and yet this one wasn't even on her radar.

"Simon told me about it," Noah said with a shrug as he took his seat.

Lucille sat beside him, leaving the seat across the table for Sylvia. She bristled at Simon giving Noah a tip he hadn't bothered to share with her. He was relentless in his attempt to get her to accept Noah.

She didn't have long to be insulted, at least not by Simon. As soon as she'd sat back in the white padded chair, the server reappeared, escorting their guest to the table.

The last time Lucille had seen Sylvia Stanton, the woman had been in rough shape. She'd faked her own kidnapping, been in hiding on Mino Island for a while, then actually kidnapped Michel and Brett. The strain of trying to force one of the men to perform a marriage ceremony between her and the other had shown on her thin, angular face. Her hair had been badly in need of a cut and dye, dirty blonde roots poking through the tangled mess. Her outfit had been a few days past fresh.

The woman who entered their secluded alcove now was a far cry from the one in the mansion. Her blonde hair shone, her contour was flawless, and the strapless white jumpsuit she wore made Lucille tense with envy. She wore huge diamond-rimmed sunglasses and strolled in looking like she owned the place and, odds were, her father actually did own it.

When she saw Lucille, however, she stopped, whipped off her glasses, and contorted her face into one of the scariest glares Lucille had ever seen, the scariest being her own, naturally. She waited until they were alone and then hissed, "You."

"Hello, Sylvia," Lucille said calmly. She'd anticipated her presence enraging the heiress and was planning to use it to her advantage. She expected to be blamed for ruining Sylvia's life, reputation, and $56,000 dress. Then use those same points to make some ground rules for their interaction. And drive up their fees. No one should have to work with Sylvia Stanton for anything less than an atrociously exorbitant amount of money.

Only Sylvia didn't follow the script Lucille had written for her. She took a deep breath, sat down at the table, crossed one leg over the other, and gave them both a dazzling smile.

Noah cleared his throat. "Sylvia, I can call you Sylvia, right?"

"If you want," she said sweetly.

"I hope you don't mind I brought Lucille along. I understand you have a history..." The way he trailed off implied he wanted them to talk about their history now and get it over with.

Sylvia shook her head, her hair tumbling around her face. "I should have put it together. You said you work with Simon Anton who of course would be related to you... I'm sorry, what's your first name again?"

The way Sylvia said it, her eyebrows slightly arched, her blue eyes a sea of concern, Lucille was deeply impressed. She'd been expecting a screaming, angry, dramatic starlet and what she'd gotten was a manipulative bitch. Lucille couldn't help herself, she was intrigued. "That was cold," she said, her voice in awe.

Sylvia looked at her, eyes glinting, her deep-red lip-sticked mouth curving into a small smile. "Thanks."

They stared at each other for a while longer, an unspoken conversation passing between them that Lucille was both not expecting and not mad about.

The server interrupted to take drink orders.

When he'd left again, Lucille said, "Sorry about the dress. I normally would never bleed all over something so exquisite."

"And then steal it and sleep with my cousin while wearing it?" Sylvia asked, her eyebrows arching higher. There was a laugh behind her voice and Lucille found herself picking up on it and smirking.

"That too," she said.

Sylvia shook her head again. "Well. I'm sorry for trying to shoot you."

"And Michel?"

Sylvia sighed. "Especially Michel. Although, it was exhausting dating that man. He's absolutely fucking perfect at everything and he's like that all. The. Time."

"It drove you mad?" Lucille suggested. Six months ago, she would never have thought she'd be having a candid, almost friendly conversation with Sylvia Stanton. Six months ago, she fully expected, and hoped, to never see the woman ever again.

"That and the drugs I was on," Sylvia said, looking down at the table.

Lucille frowned, surprised by Sylvia's cavalier confession of her drug abuse. Sure, she'd suspected it. Sylvia's actions had been exaggerated, her villainy disproportionate with reality. But had she actually gone to rehab instead of doing what so many of the rich and famous did—use rehab and mental instability as an excuse for their extralegal activities?

The drinks arrived and she found herself raising her soda water in a toast to Sylvia's cucumber-lemon water.

"What the fuck?" Noah said suddenly.

Lucille blinked at him. She hadn't forgotten he was there, exactly, but she also hadn't thought about him much in the past few minutes.

"I thought you hated each other," he continued. He looked between them, his expression incredulous.

"We did," Sylvia said with a shrug.

Lucille nodded. "Yes, but I think that's changing."

"Did someone put something in your drinks?" He frowned, his body rigid with disbelief and confusion.

Lucille turned toward him. "Can I talk to you in private for a second? Excuse us, Sylvia."

Sylvia waved them away and scanned the menu.

Lucille pulled him out into the hall. "What's going on with you?"

"Me? What going on with me? You just spent the last twenty-four hours telling me off for wanting to work with Sylvia Stanton, and now what, you're best friends with her?" Noah's face flushed as he whispered indignantly at her.

Lucille hissed back with equal indigence. "I'm not best friends with her. She just isn't as bad as I thought she'd be, okay? So, can you please stop fucking this up for me?"

She knew it sounded ridiculous. She was Lucille Anton, ice queen. She kept her clients at arm's length and everyone else further than that. She turned the term "scary bitch" into a compliment and wore it proudly. But it didn't feel ridiculous to connect with Sylvia Stanton. It felt like she'd finally found someone she could have a real friendship with, one where she didn't have to swoop in and save someone every other month like she did with the guys. Of course, it also meant Sylvia wasn't quite the ideal, train wreck of a client she'd anticipated, but maybe that was okay too.

She sighed and tried to explain it to Noah. "I get it seems weird, especially coming from me, but I think, if circumstances had been different and Sylvia hadn't been dating Michel—"

"Or taking so many drugs," Noah added.

"Or taking drugs, we could have been friends," Lucille said. In her mind, she reimagined their first meeting. She'd have run into Sylvia at a party and they'd be catty to each other for a while before bonding over their rich, fucked-up families and inability to have a healthy romantic relationship.

She sighed and looked at Noah.

His expression was something she couldn't name. The look he gave her was soft, not sympathetic but gentle. He didn't say anything, just nodded and returned to the table.

"Don't mind me, waiting here while you two go off and feel each other up in the hallway," Sylvia said as they sat down.

It was such a snarky, nasty thing to say, and Lucille laughed. "Please. There's nothing like that going on between me and Noah."

"Why not?" Sylvia asked, looking him over.

Lucille also looked him over. *Why not indeed.* "We work together. Been there, done that."

"I did hear about that. You and my cousin, I mean," Sylvia said, returning her attention to Lucille.

"You did? How? No one's heard about it."

"Oh, please, like you're the only one with sources."

On an impulse she would never be able to explain later, Lucille said, "Should we have lunch and compare notes?"

"Yes. We absolutely should."

Once again, Noah burst in to make his presence known. "Are you two going to do this all day or can we get on to the business part of the business meeting?"

Lucille raised an eyebrow at him, but he was right. Enough bonding. There was business to be done. They ordered food and Sylvia launched into her story.

After her father got her charges dropped, she'd gone to an expensive, exclusive rehab. While in rehab, she'd finally been able to detox from all the shit she'd been putting into her body. The substances, and the potent drug that was her relationship with Michel.

"When the therapist told me all the things I'd tried to do to Michel, I couldn't believe it. I mean, yes, I was capable of doing them, but I don't remember. I remember being mad at him because nothing could touch him while my life was falling apart so completely. And when I saw the video of my dad disowning me..." She shuddered.

Lucille remembered the video well. Most everyone had seen it, a dozen times at least. It trended, it lingered, it resurfaced. Sylvia and Lou Stanton fighting in a hotel lobby and Lou disowning his daughter. People had loved watching Sylvia get what they assumed she deserved.

"But that's all in the past. I'm starting over, I'm in recovery, and this is where I need your help. I need good PR and I need it now. My dad's still not convinced I'm back to my old self. I need to prove this to him or else I'm out again, no allowance, no inheritance, no nothing. I'd have to, I don't know, get a job, and I have zero marketable skills."

While Sylvia talked, Lucille's mind flew through the possibilities. The pre-Michel Sylvia Stanton had been all over the media—shopping with the girls, partying with A-listers, hosting charity events on the Stanton yacht. They needed something bigger than that, something huge.

"Reality TV show," said Noah.

Lucille stared at him. Had he read her mind? Or was he actually that good at this already? It was, of course, the best solution.

"Say what?" Sylvia asked, turning from one to the other.

"You're going to do a reality TV show. A Day in the Life of Sylvia Stanton. You'll shop, you'll host parties, you'll go to runway shows and gallery openings. You'll have an entourage of friends and frenemies and you'll show the world you're back," Noah said, leaning forward as he talked, his brown eyes bright and his words coming fast in his excitement. "Lucille, we have connections at the networks, right?"

Lucille couldn't hold back her grin and didn't want to. "Her father? Who owns three of them?"

"Right, right," said Noah.

Lucille looked at Sylvia for her reaction.

She tilted her head to the side, seeming to consider them carefully. Finally, she broke into a brilliant smile. "I love it."

Two hours, a few phone calls, and lots of martinis, on the part of Lucille and Noah, later, Sylvia Stanton had a reality show. Lucille locked down plans for their lunch and left feeling powerful and successful. She didn't even mind that Noah had had one too many martinis, snored on the way home, and appeared to be imposing on her begrudging hospitality for another night.

Chapter Thirteen

B rett's alarm went off far too early in the morning. He reached out to turn it off and found himself trapped by Michel's arm, his body pressed close, his morning erection very much present against Brett's thigh. With some difficulty, he shut off the alarm, then lay there, wondering what happened next. Was this the part where he suggested they stay in bed all day, getting to know each other's bodies and having lots of sex?

Brett's throat started closing up. He'd had sex before, not a lot in comparison to other people certainly, and never with a man, in fact, but he had experience. So why did he feel like running when presented with the opportunity to get down and dirty with Michel? Was it because Michel was a guy? No, he didn't think that was the reason for his hesitancy. It was...something else.

Michel stirred and Brett turned his head to find Michel squinting at him, an adorable frown on his face. "Morning," he said, his voice scratchy and delicious.

"Hi," Brett said, smiling. He reached his hand out and curled it in Michel's hair, digging his fingers gently against Michel's scalp. Michel made a happy little sigh and leaned into Brett's massage.

After a few moments of silence, Michel, whose face was pressed against Brett's shoulder, said in a muffled grumble, "You're not serious about this hike, are you?"

Brett wanted to say no. He wanted to say hiking was a terrible idea and he was kidding about the whole thing. They could spend their whole day wrapped up in each other just like this.

The night before rushed back at him. Almost getting it on with Michel, being called away by his sisters, the white-blonde-haired person who he definitely knew, and the huge, colossal blunder that would come back to bite him in the ass at any moment. And not the fun kind of ass bite, the very nasty, painful kind. The kind where his sisters found out he'd lied about being on a work trip and hidden his relationship, his friendship, his entire history with Michel from them. He choked down the rising bile. He needed to get Michel out of this hotel and soon.

"It's the best option to avoid my sisters."

"Fuck your sisters," Michel groaned and burrowed in closer to Brett.

"Please don't," he said, his heart pounding from the contact.

Thirty minutes later, he'd dragged Michel out of bed, avoided Michel's attempts to lure him into co-showering, and dressed in the closest thing he'd brought to a hiking outfit, that was also the only thing he'd brought—jeans and a t-shirt. As he pulled the shirt over his head, Michel walked out of the closet wearing long khaki shorts and a tight green shirt, so tight it showed the outline of his muscles. He wore sunglasses on his head and designer hiking boots, looking like he'd stepped out of the pages of *Mountaineering Magazine*.

"I thought you didn't hike?" Brett asked, captivated by the presentation.

"Always be prepared, Brett," said Michel with a wink.

"You're like a fashion boy scout."

The look Michel gave him was filled with wicked promises. Brett swallowed and turned away.

The trip out of the hotel was uneventful. Brett stayed on high alert for any sign of his sisters, but they met no one. The only unusual activity was his own as he peered around corners and declared them clear before allowing Michel to proceed. Michel indulged him.

They left the resort by a side door and found the path the hotel staff had directed Brett to the day before. Brett led the way, alternating between watching the ground beneath his feet and looking back to see if Michel was still with him. Which was ridiculous since, of the two of them, Michel was by far the more in shape and prepared for an impromptu wilderness trek.

"What is it, Brett?" Michel asked when Brett stared at him for the fifth time in a few minutes.

"I don't know," Brett said, "I guess I've never seen you do anything outdoorsy before."

"That is because I don't. Except for when I was in *Wilderness* and played the man who set out to hike the globe. On the day we wrapped, I vowed never to hike again."

"Yet here you are."

Michel raised an eyebrow at him. "Yes, here I am. I must be into you."

Brett's heart gave a flutter. He was surprised it could do that when it was trying so desperately to keep his body oxygenated during this unanticipated and unprecedented exertion. His thought again about sex. It wasn't ever far from his mind, but now it was especially at the forefront. They hadn't gone far. He could still suggest they hole up in bed all day. But no, he wasn't ready for that. And it wasn't because of his lack of experience with men, he'd established that. It was because...

Because it was too important. Michel was too important, and he needed it to be perfect because he still couldn't believe he was even with Michel. Michel, who everyone wanted to be with, who could have anyone he wanted. Who was serious and intense and untouchable. There was no casual with Michel, no falling into bed laughing and making fun of their awkward floundering the first time. There was only the jump, the fall, the deep. He needed to be more than enough—he needed to be perfect.

"You must," he responded finally and stopped, glancing back at his boyfriend. Boyfriend. What a word. He'd finally started thinking of Michel as his boyfriend, but it still felt strange in a way it shouldn't. After all, they'd agreed to be boyfriends in the car after the not-sex party, a month ago. Only, then they'd been apart for most of the month and Brett's neuroses had the chance to move in and take up residence.

He fought down all of that and focused on the challenges ahead. The path started to climb and wasn't as beautifully groomed as he'd expect for something adjacent to the elaborate resort. There were rocks and roots and little bends not yet straightened out by human intervention. Around them, the tropical trees hung low, keeping out the harshness of the morning sun. Birds chirped loudly, and an unseen creature made loud, screeching noises. Brett thought it may be a monkey, but he was no zoologist. He'd never seen so much as a nature documentary.

The path climbed up and away from The Reef. Their progress was slow going, Brett stretching it out as much as possible. He wanted to make this last, to make sure their adventure took the whole day. But their slow pace was also because of how horribly out of shape he was. That was the part he would not be sharing with Michel. Michel, who was also breathing a little heavier but in his sexy Michel way, not in the gasping, gulping manner Brett struggled for air.

He had a backpack of food, ordered from the resort staff who were only too happy to cater to their every whim. It had been waiting outside their door that morning and he had yet to so much as look inside to see what they'd packed. The last time he'd worn a backpack had been in undergrad. By grad school, he was a devote follower of the shoulder bag trend. The straps cut into his shoulders and reminded him of a time before any of this. Back when he was a normal guy, trying to pass classes, trying to figure out why he was studying science when it was so damn hard, trying to figure out if he liked boys or girls or both or if it even mattered because none of them were interested in him anyway. When he was living at home but avoiding his family, still in their clutches but with enough insight to see the dysfunction to which they'd all subscribed.

Of course, then he hadn't chosen a different path. He'd decided to give it a go, written a screenplay, immediately gotten an agent and was, for a time, the envy of the family he wanted so badly to support him. His agent, Lauren Fontile, now Cunningham, had helped him sell *The Night Before the Apocalypse* to his uncle and it was green lit almost immediately. The production was fast, wild, and wonderfully stressful. Then it was done, the movie premiered, and Brett was sent off to write the sequel. There it all stalled.

In retrospect, it was obvious Michel's move to the hills had contributed to his downward spiral. At the time, he'd thought he chased Michel away, he'd been unable to save his friend from Sylvia. Because of his failure, Michel was gone and he was alone. The drinking had a lot to do with the spiral. The excessive indulgence sanctioned, even encouraged, by his family. Then the cancelation of his contract with Stanton Enterprises, the uncle who fired him but blamed his agent, who in turn blamed Brett.

The only bright points in the whole fucking mess were Lucille and Michel. JP, too, although he didn't see the guy often, despite working at his company. He would include Simon except that Simon didn't like him and the feeling was mutual. Simon did seem to have warmed up to him now Brett wasn't dating his niece anymore. He wondered what Simon thought of Lucille and Noah's sexual tension-fueled animosity.

Finally, after what felt like forever but wasn't, the trees cleared, the path leveled, and ahead of them was the most beautiful piece of nature Brett had ever seen. They stood at the top of a translucent, pale-blue waterfall, surrounded by craggy, moss-covered rocks, rainbows dancing through the cascade as it poured into the clear pool below.

Ever since he'd given up writing, nothing had moved him to be at all creative or poetic. Nothing until this. He glanced at Michel, who'd come to stand beside him on the rocky outcrop, overlooking this vision of beauty and serenity. Sweat rolled down Michel's face as his gaze swept over the scene and he seemed as entranced by it as Brett.

Then Michel stripped off his t-shirt and shorts, and before Brett could fully react to the view, dove off the side of the waterfall.

"Michel!" Brett yelled desperately, grasping at the air too late to catch him. The pool could be too shallow, it could be covered in rocks lurking right below the surface, it might be filled with piranhas or alligators. He held his breath, fully expecting to see Michel's battered body dashed on the rocks below.

He didn't blink, transfixed by the ripples where Michel had disappeared, already preparing himself for the grief of his death. Then Michel's head bobbed up out of the water and he grinned up at Brett.

"Come on in, Brett. The water's great," Michel called over the thunder of the waterfall.

"I'm good, thanks," Brett said, pressing his hand to his chest in relief.

"Brett. You can't honestly expect me to believe you dragged us up this mountain and then aren't even going to go swimming?" Michel's voice was light and teasing.

Brett needed light and teasing. But he didn't need a broken neck from a stupid stunt.

"I'll catch you." Michel spread his arms out wide, water sliding from his skin in mesmerizing droplets.

He did want to be down there. He wanted to be near his very wet, very naked boyfriend.

"When have I ever led you astray?"

At that, Brett laughed. *Too many times to count.* He took a deep breath. *Fuck it*, he thought. After a morning of worry and crippling anxiety, he was ready to move on and just do something foolish. He stripped and dove, smacking into the pool with much more force and less grace than Michel. He sank through the clear, chilly water with a pained grunt. When he surfaced, his legs and belly stinging where they'd hit before the rest of his body, he found Michel laughing at him. He splashed Michel, who ducked. A moment later, something wrapped around his legs. He stopped himself from lashing out violently, realizing it was Michel, and instead squirmed to get out of his grasp.

Michel lifted Brett and tossed him across the pool. Brett yelled, but it was from surprise rather than terror. He soon retaliated by jumping on Michel's back and trying to dunk him. They wrestled in the cold water, scrambling for purchase on the rocky bottom, laughing and shouting like rowdy teenage boys. The wrestling inevitably turned to kissing, their hot mouths pulling at each other even as the rest of their bodies grew numb.

After their swim, they lay out on the rocks at the top of the falls, drying and eating the lunch the hotel had packed in the afternoon heat. For the first time in a long time, Brett felt only joy. No worry, no anxiety in these brief moments when he had Michel all to himself and they had this magical place, away from the concerns of the outside world.

Then he remembered they had to hike back and the mood died pretty quickly after that.

It was early evening when they began the trek down the mountain, driven by the need for rest and dinner. They didn't talk much on the return journey. Hell, they hadn't talked much the whole day, not about the things that mattered. Brett knew it was because he was hiding too many secrets. He didn't know what Michel was thinking or why he seemed to accept the silence that was so atypical of their relationship. He wasn't going to ask because he couldn't risk Michel asking questions in return. So, they walked back, the only breaks in the silence their occasional remarks about avoiding rocks and requests for water.

Half a lifetime later, the resort came into view. Brett imagined their trip back to the room, sneaking in the side door and heading straight upstairs. He'd call room service and order dinner. Then, while they were eating, he'd bring up leaving the next day so they didn't have to sneak around, avoiding his sisters. Michel would be disappointed but understand. Maybe they could go on a real romantic getaway soon, he'd say, one without the constant threat of family interruption. Brett would nod, his throat closed off, his afternoon courage gone and his feeling of deep inadequacy growing.

Lost in imagining, it took Brett too long to notice the people lounging outside the side door. When they'd left, there hadn't been seating in this area of the resort. It was a small, landscaped perimeter that quickly dropped off into rocks and plant life. Now, squished into the tiny space, were two chairs and a small table, on which sat two enormous, fruit garnished pina coladas. And in the chairs, lounging as though they were prepared to wait all night, were the very last people he wanted to see. His sisters.

His phone buzzed. It was a text from an unknown number, a blocked number. *You're welcome* was all it said.

CHAPTER FOURTEEN

After Lucille unloaded the sleeping Noah into the guest room, she settled at her desk to put in a few more hours of work. She'd barely opened her computer when her phone announced an incoming video call. Seeing it was Simon, she answered.

Simon's face filled the screen, giving her a close-up of his meticulously wrinkle-free skin. "What's this I hear about you becoming friends with Sylvia Stanton?" he asked by way of a greeting.

Lucille was never surprised when Simon knew things he couldn't possibly know. But she found the habit annoying, particularly in this case because his informant had to have been Noah. "Did he text you or something?" She didn't bother to explain who she meant.

"As I've told you many times, Lucy, the way I got the information is not important—"

"Did he?"

"Yes."

Lucille raised an eyebrow at her uncle. She had her phone propped in a holder as she scrolled through her email, looking for interesting subject lines. "You can't honestly think I'd tell you about a meeting with a client."

It was another of Simon's rules of spin doctoring—never tell people you care about what you're doing.

"No, but now I know and, I repeat, you're friends with Sylvia Stanton?" Simon was walking somewhere, most likely around his house. He wouldn't be talking this openly if he were anywhere he could be overheard.

"I don't like this, Noah texting you about my meetings."

"He's my protégé."

"I never texted you what I was doing when I was your protégé," Lucille wasn't about to let this go.

Simon glared at her. Then he broke. "Okay, fine. I never asked Noah to text me, he just does it. He's into this working-together thing. And since he's keeping me informed of your budding friendship with Sylvia, I'm disinclined to reprimand him about just yet."

Lucille laughed. "I hate to burst your bubble, but your so-called protégé is currently sleeping off his day drinking in my guest room."

Simon continued to glare at her. "Oh, please, like you've never done that."

She was about to say she hadn't but then remembered that one time when she'd been a young spin doctor, still learning the trade, and she'd slammed a pitcher of margaritas to impress a new client. The client had been impressed. Her stomach had not.

She rolled her eyes. "Yes, fine. Sylvia isn't who I thought she was. Turns out, when she's not dating Michel and taking a bunch of drugs, she's actually a cold and calculating bitch."

"Surprising," said Simon, his glare finally dissipating now he'd gotten what he wanted.

"I thought so."

"In that case, send me back my protégé." He paused. "Unless you want to keep him?"

It was her turn to glare. "As soon as he's not comatose, he'll be on the next plane back to you."

She hung up. For some reason, all the men, possibly with the exception of Michel since she hadn't spoken to him directly in a bit, were intent on making her and Noah a thing. Which, now she wasn't angry with him, she didn't hate.

The facts were these:

Noah was hot.

He could keep up with her, at least in the business side of things.

The moment from the club when she'd told him off and he'd been turned on was burned into her memory. It was just possible Noah Harkin had a bit of a submissive streak, a quality that would pair well with her controlling streak.

They could be good together.

Lucille tried to put it out of her mind and focus on the work in front of her. Just because she'd spent the afternoon away from the news didn't mean the news stopped. New scandals were always on the horizon and where and how they broke had to be under her control.

Her mind wandered back to Noah.

She pulled it back as she spied a text from Brett. A text that wiped everything else from her mind. His sisters had found out about Michel. They were annoying, sure, and would require more than a little bribery and misdirection to leave Michel and Brett alone. The unknown number, though... Brett was right, someone seemed to be orchestrating this fiasco. Someone sneaky. Someone whose motivations and end game weren't clear but who was evidently intent on doing something to Brett. Well, that someone didn't know he had Lucille on his side.

She copied the unknown number and sent it to JP. For a moment, she wondered what JP thought of his new role as official celebrity spin doctor call tracer. She doubted he approved.

The door of her office had been ajar and now swung all the way open, revealing Noah, still in his somehow unwrinkled suit. He squinted, even though the sun was setting and she hadn't turned on a light. "What's going on?" he asked, his voice scratchy with sleep.

Lucille set her phone down. She didn't know how Noah had managed to keep his suit pristine through his drunken nap, but she liked it. "I'm working," she said, stopping the conversation before it could begin.

Noah yawned, nodded, and left. Lucille turned back to her computer.

Less than a minute later, Noah was back with his laptop and a chair. "Can I work in here with you?" he asked his voice adorably hopeful.

It was her turn to blink at him. She didn't share her workspace. Or at least, no one had ever wanted to share it with her. And yet, her desk was large, there was plenty of room, and she could focus through anything. Before she could remind herself not to let him get too comfortable, she nodded and moved her tablet to make room.

He pulled up his chair, set up his computer, and zeroed in at once. Silence returned to the office. But it didn't matter that he didn't talk. It didn't matter how focused he was on his work. He was destroying her concentration. She couldn't stop thinking about the what-ifs and the why-nots. There was the big one—they worked together. But she already worked with her uncle, how different would be it working with a boyfriend? No. *Definitely not a boyfriend*, she thought with a grimace. A guy she was fucking? Better.

She was the one who broke the silence. Desperate for anything to make him less appealing to her, she asked, "Now you've seen how actual celebrity spin doctoring works, I imagine you're going to give up these retrieval mission schemes."

Noah's head jerked up when she started talking, his hands paused on the keyboard. "Why?"

Lucille's hands stilled on her own keyboard. "Because they're dangerous and unnecessary. Why would we go through the whole process of retrieving the flash drive when we could convince everyone the flash drive doesn't exist or is a fake?"

Noah studied her, his head tilted to one side. "You would be excellent at PI work, you know that?"

Lucille glared back at him.

"No, seriously, like the crime club party when you were the sex toy consultant? Brilliant. And that outfit...no offense red suit, but that outfit was smoking."

She couldn't read him, and it was frustrating. "That was a onetime thing and it was a crisis."

The crisis being Simon was supposed to be keeping an eye on Michel, but had let him run off and join a group of dangerous celebrity criminals as "character research."

Noah shook his head. "No, see, I think where we've gone wrong so far is in the approach. I say we work smarter not harder."

She suspected he was messing with her.

He went on. "From now on, we send you in undercover. You can pretend to be a sex consultant or stripper or whatever and get the incriminating evidence without having to break into anything."

She *knew* he was messing with her. "You're full of shit."

"I am, but so are you," he replied calmly.

"What the fuck are you talking about?"

"Your attitude, Lucille. We might not have known each other long, but I do know this. Whenever you think someone's getting too close, you start acting like a superior asshole to push them away again."

She frowned at him. A real frown, full eyebrow wrinkle and everything. *Excuse me?*

Nothing he said was news to her. She did push people away, always had and frankly, always would. People who thought they could bust through her armor and get close to her without her wanting them to. But Noah saw her invisible defenses, saw them but didn't ask to cross them— *Shit.*

"You know, that's not a terrible plan. What are you thinking, I'll seduce the ones with the evidence into giving it to me? Maybe have sex with some of them? I mean, not everyone is going to fall for some light stripping. I might have to go all the way and might as well enjoy myself even if it is for work—"

Noah cut her off. "All right, all right. You made your point. I'll back off."

Lucille gave him a sweet smile. "Good."

He frowned down at his hands. If she didn't know better, she'd say he was a little jealous. She'd also say she liked him being a little jealous. And, where Noah was concerned, she was beginning to suspect she didn't know as much as she thought she did.

"My way is more exciting, you have to admit," he said, his expression clearing again. Whatever he'd felt during her teasing had been pushed aside.

"Fine. I'll give you that." She turned her attention back to the computer.

"And," Noah began and paused. He paused for so long she looked at him. His eyes held a mischievous expression. "I hear you're excellent at climbing walls in knee-high boots."

Lucille couldn't believe it. Was anything secret? Apparently not between Simon and Noah. And yet Simon hadn't bothered to tell Noah all the reasons he shouldn't work with Sylvia? Back when there were reasons not to work with her and good ones at that, of course. "I'm going to kill Simon."

"Do you still have those boots?" he asked, clearly faking innocent curiosity.

"No," Lucille said.

"Too bad."

She didn't agree. The boots had been terribly designed and constructed. The only reason she'd been wearing them was to get Beverly Walton talking and she'd fully intended to burn them at the end of the night. But that was, again, not the point. "Don't you have a plane to catch? The Sylvia case is under control, so there's no need to hang around."

Noah shook his head carefully. "Nope. Can't fly until this hangover is gone."

Lucille let out a deep, audible sigh. "Well. Then just sit over there and work quietly."

She hadn't meant to snap so forcefully, not that Noah didn't deserve it.

She also wasn't prepared for his response. At her command, his whole body seemed to relax and interest flared briefly in his eyes, just like it had at the club and when she'd ordered him around in the kitchen. Then it was gone.

Lucille forced herself back to the gossip blogs, forced herself to remember she had a job to do and it didn't involve seeing what else would bring out that reaction in her all-too-sexy coworker.

They fell silent again, the only sound the clatter of keyboard keys and the click of the mouse. Without thinking, she found herself on a BDSM site she'd heard about. She was under no illusions she knew anything about BDSM, having gained what she did know from secondhand stories of the Deviant Club. And she wasn't sure she was into it, nor that Noah was into it, but it couldn't hurt to do some research, could it? After all, she hadn't imagined those reactions of his. Her own desire grew, tangible and right below the surface, waiting for one of them to give in.

If the next events had gone differently, there was a strong possibility they'd have ended up in bed before the evening was out.

It began about an hour later with a text from JP. *You all do know I'm not your personal phone tracker?*

That solved the mystery of what JP thought of his role in their less than legal activities. *The person who has this phone is out to get Brett. They may be behind Brett's sisters vacationing on the same island at the same time as Brett and Michel.*

Ok...so they're having a little Jacobs family re-union.

Lucille rolled her eyes. Of course, Simon wouldn't have said anything to JP about Brett's family. *One of Brett's sisters is the president of the largest Michel Polce fan club in the world. The other wrote Under-neath the Glamor Lies Nothingness.*

This did the trick. JP, in his knowledge of nerdy pop culture, could no doubt imagine the potential damage a fan club president could do to the subject of the fandom. And of course, he'd heard of Patience Jacobs's book. Anyone even remotely related to anything to do with the celebrity world knew about her eviscerating, supposedly fictional account of a star's decline into nothingness. *Ah. Yikes.*

Brief pause and then another text. *I'll do what I can. But if it's not an LT Tech phone there's not a lot I can do.*

Lucille had every faith in JP's capabilities. Before he was co-CEO of one of the largest technology companies worldwide, he'd been a programmer with genius-level hacker abilities. *Thank you.*

She put her phone down.

"What's that about?" Noah asked.

She found him watching her and realized she'd been smiling and making expressions at her phone during the exchange. For a moment, she considered telling him it had nothing to do with him, which was what she would have told Simon. But Noah was supposed to be learning, and she might as well teach him the correct way to handle situations. "JP is going to trace a phone number for me."

Noah looked more curious than ever. "Didn't he say he wasn't, under any circumstances, going to do any more illegal phone tracing for us?"

"Yes, well, this is a bit of an unusual situation," she said.

Noah waited.

Lucille sighed, ignored her instinct to keep everything to herself, and told Noah all about Brett, Brett's sisters, and the anonymous text. She leaned back in her chair as she spoke, one leg crossed over the other, staring absently at the ceiling.

When she finished talking, she looked down at Noah. He had an odd expression on his face. Almost like her story caused him pain. Which was ridiculous since it had nothing to do with him and everything to do with her best friend being a neurotic idiot.

"Brett. As in Sylvia's cousin Brett? The one she said you hooked up with?" he asked the questions slowly, carefully.

Now Lucille was confused, an unnatural feeling for her. "Yeah, we dated for a while—"

"You dated Sylvia's cousin? The guy who's now on a romantic getaway with Michel Polce?"

What the hell?

He continued. "When did this happen?"

"When did what happen?" she asked, not to be obtuse but because she couldn't see where this line of questioning was going.

"The dating, Lucille."

"Why do you care?"

"I just do."

She wasn't about to accept that as the full answer. If he was going to act like a jealous nutcase, he'd better be upfront about it.

Noah huffed. "Fine. Were you still dating Brett when we made out?"

Was that what this whole thing was about? Noah wanted to know if she'd cheated on Brett with him? "We'd broken up," she said, feeling the entire argument was silly and childish. And not a little insulting. "Brett's my best friend. I can't believe you think I'd do that to him."

"That's not..." He trailed off and ran a hand through his hair. "I honestly don't know what you're capable of."

Whatever sexual tension Lucille had been picking up on was gone. She stood and grabbed her phone. She could defend herself and say she'd never hurt the people she loved. Or she could pry into Noah's character and try to find something she could accuse him of the way he was accusing her. She could explain how she and Brett had a fast and fierce fling that burned out quickly but left behind a surprisingly close friendship. She could confess old Lucille might have kissed someone to keep them quiet, regardless of her relationship status. The Lucille who'd been abandoned and betrayed by everyone close to her, before she'd found friends and family and her purpose. If he thought she was capable of cheating now, he should have met her then.

She didn't say any of it. In a curt voice that clearly communicated she was done with this conversation, she said, "Good night," and left the room.

If Noah responded, she didn't hear him.

CHAPTER FIFTEEN

There had been a total of three times in his life when Brett honestly hoped the ground would open beneath his feet and swallow him whole. The first was in high school when he'd been trying to fit in with his family and some of his terrible poetry got out and made the rounds of mockery. The second happened when Michel told him he was not only dating Brett's cousin Sylvia, but they were also moving in together and away from Brett. The third was this moment right now.

Maybe he could move underground, coming out once a year to blink in the sunlight and refresh his stock of soda and canned soup. Anything to keep this meeting from happening, to keep himself from being in it.

"Brett, what the fuck are you doing?" Evelyn called to him as he stood frozen in horror, torn between staring at his siblings and at the mysterious text on his phone.

His sisters. He was returning from a gloriously romantic day with Michel and there, where no table and chairs had been before, were his sisters. Patience, decked in a vast, flowing number, covered all over in toucans and bright-blue palm trees, and looking like someone had attacked her with color, eyed him mildly. Evelyn, who stared at him like he was the crazy one, wore a sarong over her bedazzled bikini and, even from a distance, Brett could smell the coconut oil sunscreen on her skin.

As he froze, he imagined possible scenarios. Since the ground wasn't cooperating in swallowing him whole, he would have to save Michel himself. He could leap in front of him or push him into the ocean, or throw something at his sisters to distract them from him, or...

It was too late. Michel wasn't far behind him, and he stopped next to Brett. Although Brett had successfully kept him away from meeting his family, he knew Michel recognized his sisters. After all, he'd been hounded by Evelyn before, in her role of fan club president, and there was a mounting pile of evidence identifying him as one of the characters in Patience's book.

Brett saw the moment Evelyn noticed Michel. Saw her waving arm fall, saw her mouth drop open, her eyes flicker wildly between Brett and Michel, her struggle to breathe. He saw Patience narrow her eyes, her body tense and ready to spring. And then there was Michel, dear sweet Michel, who knew the vipers were out and there was nothing to stop them from attacking.

"Your sisters," Michel said softly, his voice mild but betraying a hint of trepidation.

Brett stared at Michel, his face blank, his brain slow to process. He wasn't handling this well. He'd known the meeting was a possibility and yet was completely and utterly unprepared.

"Hello, Michel," Evelyn breathed, finally able to speak. Her face was hungry.

"Hello again, Evelyn," Michel replied in the calm voice he used around his more extreme fans.

"I haven't seen you since the *Seasons of Light* premiere. You haven't been anywhere."

Michel said, in his most press-ready tone, "I've been taking some time to myself before I research my next role. You'll see plenty of me in the coming months when I start doing promo for the new film."

"Taking some time to yourself...with our brother?" Patience asked, her voice loud, cutting through the rush in Brett's ears.

"Yes, in fact, I have been." The way Michel spoke, his voice so definitive, so certain, should have anchored Brett. It didn't.

"Fascinating," said Patience, raising one eyebrow. "Is it?"

Evelyn jumped in. "Oh, my God, Brett. How dare you keep him all to yourself. I can't believe he's been here this whole time and you didn't tell us. Mom'll be furious. I wouldn't be surprised if she disowns you for real this time, you little shit."

That was part one of her speech. The second part involved her jumping out of her chair, grabbing Michel by the arm, and demanding he come with her to the bar where they could sit and have a chat. "I may never forgive my brother, but don't worry, I'd never be mad at you. You already know you're my idol, but I just have to say, I love every little thing about you, and I need to hear everything. When did you lose your first tooth? When did you get your driver's license? Oh, and I'll need a list of all the people you've kissed..."

The door closed as she dragged Michel through it. Patience followed close behind, looking delighted at the turn of events.

Brett stood outside alone, looking after them and blinking. "What the hell just happened?" he asked no one.

He considered going back up to the waterfall and leaping off the edge. But it was too long a hike. He thought about going back up to the room and hiding in a corner until Michel came back and broke up with him. But he couldn't do that to Michel. It was his family and, while he'd long ago gotten over feeling responsible for their disfunction, he was going to protect Michel from them as best he could.

He found the group at a high-top table between the pool and the bar. Michel was stuck between Evelyn and Patience, who flanked him so closely they looked like they were holding him hostage. Fortunately, it was dinner time and the bar was deserted apart from their group. Brett was grateful for the lack of witnesses.

He drew a chair up to the high-top table just in time to hear Evelyn ask, "How often do you secretly date fans?"

Michel looked up when Brett sat down. His face had turned from a mask of calm to uncomfortable confusion.

"Evelyn," Brett cut in, "really? Michel doesn't have to tell you about his dating history."

"I already know most of it. I just want to fill in the rest, the stuff no one knows. I mean you're obviously close to my brother, and I'm related to him. So, it's like telling family," Evelyn said, leaning closer, if possible, to Michel. She was practically in his lap, bedazzled bikini top pressed against his arm, entirely oblivious to Michel's visible discomfort.

"They're dating," Patience said. She scrutinized Michel in a very different way than Evelyn. Evelyn was soaking in Michel, giddy to the point where she seemed in danger of passing out with excitement. Patience was watching him as someone stares at a new species, noting its markings, trying to understand how it lives.

"What?" Evelyn screeched.

Michel flinched away from her.

"I mean, I'd heard there were rumors you had a thing going on with a guy, but my brother? Like seriously, my brother?" Evelyn's voice rose.

"Thanks," Brett mumbled. His face was red and so hot he might spontaneously combust.

"She has a point," Patience said. "You make an unlikely couple."

Michel jumped in at this point. "That's not a nice thing to say about your brother. I happen to like him quite a lot."

Maybe Brett could drown in the pool. It was convenient, close by, and he would definitely be able to get Evie to hold his head down until the bubbles stopped.

Evelyn laughed. It wasn't a nice laugh, it was a fucking scary laugh. "That's only because you haven't spent much time with the other Jacobs. I promise you, Brett is completely atypical for our family. He's the black sheep no one talks about anymore. Now, if you want to spend the rest of your trip with me, I'd be happy to help you forget all about him."

Her words were so cold, so cliché, they seemed unreal. Who talked about their family like that? His did. His family talked about him like that all the time. If anything had changed since the days when he'd been so desperate for their attention, it wasn't them. In that instant, when he felt smaller than nothing, Brett wasn't sure it was him either. They would always be the people whose barbs he couldn't shake off, the ones who got under his skin no matter how hard he fought to keep them out.

Evelyn had herself wrapped around Michel's arm. Patience didn't contradict Evie's words, didn't stick up for Brett at all.

And Evelyn wasn't done. "Okay, but seriously, Michel. Let's look at all the people you've dated and then compare them to Brett. Patience, get another round, this could take a while."

Brett couldn't look at Michel. Tears pricked at the back of his eyes. This was absolutely the end. He didn't hear if Michel responded, he simply got up, turned, and started to walk away. Before he'd made it a few steps, Patience stopped him. For a second, the briefest of seconds, he thought she was going to apologize and denounce the horrible things Evelyn had said. But this was Patience.

"Brett. I'm only saying this because I'm looking out for you. Do you even know what you're doing?"

"What are you talking about?" As if he didn't know.

"This is Michel Polce. You don't really think you two are in the same league, do you? He'll drop your ass as soon as he realizes you're not enough, you know that, right? It's the social order." She spoke in what she probably thought was a concerned tone but, like all of Patience, it was devoid of actual feeling.

Brett couldn't respond. He wanted to tell her she was wrong, wanted to believe she was wrong. But he couldn't. So, he pushed past her and hurried inside, desperate to get back to the room before the tears started.

At the door to the suite, the room where he'd had so many almosts with Michel, Brett felt a hand on his arm. He looked up, startled, to see Michel beside him, his face hard. Michel dug in the pocket of his khaki shorts, pulled out a room key, and opened the door, guiding Brett inside. Brett didn't protest when Michel closed the door behind them, didn't react when Michel steered him to the couch, and sat when Michel pushed down on his shoulders.

"I'm sorry our avoidance plan failed. I wish it had worked."

Brett glanced up and met Michel's beautiful, calm gaze that was watching him with so much open empathy. "What?"

"Your family's fucking nuts, Brett."

"What?" Brett said again, with more energy behind it. He heard Michel, but the words didn't make any sense.

"Your family. I understand now why you never wanted me to meet them, as your family, that is. They're not nice to you. I can't believe some of the things they said to me. Is that how it always is?" Michel's face was so set, so serious. The only time Brett had seen his friend that serious was when he was hard at work on an idea of his own. Not one of the coffee table books or the roles he couldn't say no to. The projects that were his, that mattered to him, and that he owned completely. Now Michel was looking at him like Brett was one of those projects. As though Michel didn't know if what he was saying was right but he needed to say it because he cared so deeply.

Brett's heart swelled. It hurt all the way up his esophagus and lodged in his throat. He looked down, blinking hard so he didn't cry. He didn't know what to say. Michel had asked him if it was always that bad. Brett didn't know how to tell him sometimes it was worse. When his parents were there, maybe an aunt thrown into the mix. He didn't have to even get into the Stanton side of the family,

Michel already knew they were a whole extra special brand of fucked up.

"Brett," Michel's voice was soft.

Brett couldn't look at him or risk blubbing. Without overthinking it, he got up and crossed the room to where Michel stood, his arms hanging at his sides as though he didn't know what to do with them or how to respond. Brett didn't stop when he reached his boyfriend. As Michel's lips parted, probably to ask something, Brett was there, his mouth crushing into Michel's. He wrapped an arm around him, feeling the heat of his body and taking comfort that Michel was real, Michel was present, and Michel cared about him.

Their kisses grew more frantic, hard and desperate. Michel's arms wrapped around him, his hands gripping Brett's ass and pulling them tightly together. Brett moaned as his erection bumped into Michel's. He couldn't help it, he rocked into it, pushing against him until Michel gasped and groaned deliciously into Brett's mouth. Brett tightened his hands in his hair. He kissed like he was trying to completely meld them together. And perhaps he was.

They were wearing too many clothes. With a reluctant grunt, Brett pulled backward. Michel's swollen, red lips chased him, but he held firm.

Without a word, he detached himself, grabbed Michel's hand, and led him into the bedroom of their suite. Then he turned to face him and pulled off his t-shirt.

"Are you sure?" Michel asked, breathing heavily.

Brett nodded. "I want this. I want you."

Michel's gaze was heavy, his hair mussed from Brett's hands, his cock visibly straining even in his hiking shorts. He followed Brett's lead, removing his shirt and then starting in on his pants.

It was forever and no time at all before they were standing naked in front of each other. Brett couldn't help it, he stared. He'd seen Michel mostly naked the last time they were on Mino, hell, everyone had seen Michel in his Speedo then, but he'd also been out of his mind with pain and booze. Now he wasn't drunk with a dislocated shoulder. Now he could stare at Michel's heart-stoppingly gorgeous body in clear, sober awe. "Holy Jesus fucking Christ," he whispered.

Michel was light-brown, muscular, with a sprinkling of dark hair that led in a perfect trail down to his cock. All thoughts Brett may have entertained about not being into dicks evaporated because it didn't matter. What mattered was that he was very, *very* into Michel's dick and wanted desperately for it to get to know his own.

After gawking for far too long, he looked up at Michel's face and found his wonder and lust mirrored there.

"I share your sentiment," Michel said, his voice deep and his accent more pronounced.

Brett laughed awkwardly. "As if. I mean all of this"—he gestured to his imperfect body— "in no way compares."

Michel shook his head. He stepped closer until he was right in front of Brett, so close their dicks could almost touch. "Don't say that. You're extraordinary."

Brett's breath caught. His heart beat wildly, and he looked at his best friend and lover with what he knew to be naked emotion. Michel leaned forward and they kissed, a brief, soft flutter of a kiss before Michel was gone. Brett's eyelids opened in time for him to see Michel settle in on his knees in front of him. The next moment, Michel's talented hands were on Brett's erection, followed closely by his mouth.

Brett gasped. He wanted to close his eyes, to revel in the sensation, but he also wanted to watch, in case he was dreaming. He looked down and nearly came on the spot. The sight of Michel's beautiful face, his mouth open as he licked and sucked, his eyes focused on his task, his body taut with pleasure and anticipation, was too much. It took all of his willpower not to fall over the edge. He kept his hands clenched at his sides until Michel guided them into his hair and Brett resumed his erotic scalp massage.

After a few minutes, Brett gave Michel's shoulders a gentle push. Michel pulled off him with a loud pop that was primal and had Brett on edge all over again. "Wait," he managed to say.

Michel, too, was gasping. "For what?"

Brett didn't know how to bring up anal. With women, he said he wanted to be inside them or wanted to have sex. But how did it work with another guy? Who asked to fuck whom? He'd thought about Michel being inside him and he was very into the idea. He'd masturbated to it. But maybe Michel wanted to be fucked?

This all lasted at most ten seconds before Brett realized it was okay. This was Michel. It didn't matter if he said the words wrong. He trusted Michel completely. "I don't want to come until one of us is balls deep in the other's ass."

Michel, who'd sat back on his heels, chuckled. Then he seemed to consider Brett.

Brett waited, his dick growing cold and his nerves starting to rise again.

"Have you been with a man, Brett?" Michel asked finally.

Brett shook his head. He didn't know where this was going. Was Michel questioning Brett's attraction to him? Or his sexual experience?

Michel simply nodded. "Do you have any desire to be fucked?"

This time, Brett nodded. His face grew hot. It was vulnerable, standing naked in front of his lover, talking about what he wanted. "Yes. I want you to fuck me."

Michel smiled. His eyes sparkled. "Interesting. As fun as that's going to be, I think you should fuck me tonight. It's going to take some work to get you ready, and I'm afraid I'm rather impatient right now."

Not that anyone would have been able to tell. Michel spoke so calmly, the heat radiating through his voice and lighting Brett up inside.

In one graceful move, Michel stood and strolled to his suitcase. He unzipped a pocket and removed a bottle of lube and a couple of condoms. These he threw on the bed before settling on the comforter on his back, his knees bent, feet apart, and everything on display.

Brett's nerves were gone. In its place was a raging fire of lust and desire. He didn't need to be asked to join Michel on the bed. In a moment, he was there, kissing Michel all over, fisting his cock, sucking his fingers, and trailing them down to Michel's hole. He might not have had sex with a man before, but he knew how to do his research, and he had. Men needed to be opened, liberally, and Brett took his time prepping Michel.

"Brett," Michel finally panted out, "I know you like to do things thoroughly, but you're killing me. Please get on with it."

Brett had never heard Michel beg for anything, and it tickled him that Michel was begging for *him*. He slipped on one of the condoms and covered them both with lube. Then he pushed in, slowly, taking his guidance from Michel's body, from his gasping cries for more.

When they were fully connected, Brett leaned over until they were face-to-face. "Hi," he said nervously, wondering if he was doing this right.

"Brett," Michel said, his calm voice containing a small edge of irritation in it. "If you don't fuck me hard right now, I will never forgive you."

Brett laughed, his nerves retreating again, and set about making Michel's request a reality. Soon, he wasn't laughing anymore, he was so caught up in the building sensations. Michel reached for his cock and, with a few slight jerks, he came. Brett followed, unable to hold on any longer. He came hard, so hard he swore he blacked out briefly.

Then he was back in the hotel room, his body falling against Michel's—sticky, sweaty, and exhausted. He clung to Michel and felt Michel clinging back to him. It took all his energy to raise his head and meet Michel's lips. They kissed. It was clumsy and sloppy but exactly what he needed. He looked down into Michel's eyes, his languid, sleepy eyes. "Can we just stay like this forever?"

A smile spread across Michel's face. "I'd like that."

A few minutes passed as they lay there, catching their breath and drifting back to reality, however reluctantly. Then their bodies began to cool and Brett reluctantly got up to take care of the mess. He climbed back into bed, and Michel, who had scooted under the covers, wrapped himself around Brett and gave the most contented sigh Brett had ever heard. He ran his fingers through Michel's hair and told himself not to think about how much sex they could have been having were it not for his hang-ups.

Finally, he spoke because he had to ask. "Michel?"

"Hmm?"

"Are you sure you're not mad about what happened with my sisters?" It was a stupid question. He shouldn't bring up his family when they were butt naked, curled around each other, coming down from an incredible high.

Michel lifted his head from where he'd laid it on Brett's chest. He scooted up the bed until they were at eye level. Brett turned his head and found Michel watching him, his brown eyes concerned. "I'm mad...at them. None of what they said is true, and I need you to believe that."

As Michel spoke, he raised a hand and laid it against Brett's cheek, giving him a gentle caress. Brett leaned into that hand, wanting all the contact he could get.

"I do, mostly."

"I get it." Michel was quiet for a while before he said, "You're not the only one with a dysfunctional family."

Brett frowned as he realized, "I don't know anything about your family."

Michel nodded. "Which is purposeful. And for the best. I have my reasons for not wanting you to have to meet them, just like you have your reasons for keeping your family away from me. Which, thank God, you did."

Brett searched Michel's eyes and saw his earnestness, understanding, and a hint of pain. "I don't want to make you talk about something you don't want to, but there's no way your family can be worse. I mean, my sister is the president of your fan club. And what's worse, it's the club my mother founded. My mother."

He grimaced just thinking about it. It was bad enough when his mother and sister were extreme fans of his friend Michel. It was far worse now it was his boyfriend they were obsessed with. Of all the people in the Jacobs family, the only person who should be obsessed with Michel, in a totally normal way, was him and him alone.

Michel laughed. "I can't believe it took me so long to realize Evelyn Jacobs is your sister."

"Maybe because I'm so damn charming and she's not?"

Michel punched him lightly in the bicep.

"Hey," Brett protested. He stopped when Michel leaned forward and lightly kissed the spot he'd punched, running his lips over Brett's sweaty skin.

Then Michel pulled back. Brett started to complain but stopped when he saw the frown on

Michel's face. "Did you ever read the Guinness Book of World Records?"

"Sometimes, yes," Brett said, also frowning. He didn't know what this had to do with anything except that it was distracting them from more kissing.

Michel rolled onto his back and looked up at the ceiling. His chest fell as he let out a long sigh. "The man with the world record of hot dogs eaten in three minutes is my dad."

Brett blinked, not sure how to respond to that.

Michel went on, "My mother has been voted the most devoted volunteer of her church group for five years straight when I was growing up. They live in this tiny little town that would not be okay with the swearing in my films, let alone accept you and me. It's probable I have younger siblings, but I left as soon as I could and haven't been back."

Silence.

"Damn," Brett said after a while. "I always pictured you having some big Italian family where everyone's hanging out together and throwing huge parties. I thought you didn't talk about them because they were intrusive and embarrassing and called you up to ask you why you had to get naked in so many of your movies."

Michel laughed. "I might have one of those somewhere. I was adopted from an orphanage in Italy when I was a kid and I never knew who my birth parents were."

Brett thought his heart would burst. He thought of Michel as a young, lonely kid with such talent and dreams, trapped in a world that didn't understand or appreciate him. Here he was, thinking he knew everything about Michel, but there was this whole part of him, this childhood that he had left behind and buried.

He scooted over until he was right next to Michel, looking down at him. His face was raw, his eyes shiny, his hair messier than Brett had ever seen it. With his free hand, Brett reached out and smoothed his hair, loving that it was his fingers that made it messy in the first place. He trailed his hand down, tracing his features, spending an extra-long time on his lips. Then he leaned in and kissed Michel gently on his kiss-swollen mouth. He poured his empathy into that kiss. His comfort for the child Michel had been, the scared kid he had to leave behind.

When he broke away, he said, feeling it for the first time, "We're going to be okay, you and me. We're going to be okay."

Michel gazed up at him and nodded, then he grabbed Brett by the neck and pulled him in for another kiss.

Chapter Sixteen

Lucille wasn't going to be the first to apologize for last night. For one thing, Noah was being a complete and utter dick about her relationship with Brett. He'd accused her of cheating on Brett, which she'd never do to Brett. He was her best friend and her favorite ex-boyfriend. Of course, there wasn't much competition but still. She and Brett may have ended their romantic relationship, but that didn't have to mean one of them cheated.

She lay in bed, scrolling through the emails and texts that populated overnight. Clients who'd done stupid shit and were desperate for her immediate help. Clients who'd been ghosting her for weeks and now needed her because they'd accidentally hooked up with a stripper the night before their wedding. And the usual twenty stream-of-conscious-ness texts from one former client about why she'd be better off without Lucille.

Maybe she should forward some of the obnoxious ones to Noah. If he was serious about being part of the team, he needed to start pulling his weight. Yes, that was what she'd do. Go wake up Noah and tell him there was work to be done, completely ignoring everything that had happened between them like the goddamn professional she was.

She threw on a silk bathrobe, not bothering to add any more clothes and not thinking much of it until she was in the guest room, standing over a mostly naked, sleeping Noah, her hands on her hips and a no-nonsense expression on her face. "Noah," she said. "Noah, wake up. We've got work to do."

His eyes opened and then he startled awake, the sheet falling away to reveal him in nothing but a pair of black boxer briefs. He stared at her and then ran his gaze over her bathrobe. "Good morning," he said, making a weak attempt to cover himself with a sheet.

Lucille huffed. "Oh, please. I couldn't care less that you're mostly naked. Our clients have had a busy night of being total fuck-ups and we need to fix it."

She pivoted on her bare feet and started a superb stalk out of the bedroom, only to be caught off guard by Noah's next words.

"I'm sorry."

"What?" She froze but didn't look back at him.

A rustle of sheets, and then Noah's hand on her arm, gently turning her toward him. She followed but kept her face impassive and unyielding.

"I had no right to comment on your relationship with Brett. I shouldn't have assumed you were still dating him when you kissed me." Noah's gaze was intense as he looked at her and she was glad once again they were the same height so he wasn't looking down at her.

"No, you shouldn't have. Because we weren't," Lucille said. Why was she explaining this to him? She knew why but hell if she was going to admit it.

"No," he said, shaking his head. "I have a whole sob story about my past relationships and why I jumped to that conclusion, but that's not what I want to do right now."

She shouldn't ask. She knew he was baiting her and asking would only lead to... "What do you want to do, Noah?"

His brown eyes, still sleepy around the edges, didn't leave hers. Slowly, deliberately, he bit his bottom lip. "Do I have to spell it out?"

She stared at him and he stared back. The temperature of the room rose at an alarming rate as they stood close together, almost naked, almost touching.

Lucille made the first move. She couldn't, wouldn't deny it was her who closed the gap and claimed Noah's lips in a hard, bruising kiss. She grabbed his hips, digging in her nails as she devoured his mouth. One of his hands was in her hair and the other was on her shoulder, ready to either push away from her or to feel her up under her robe. He gasped against her mouth as she pulled him toward her, and his erection bumped her thigh. Lucille ate his gasp and rocked hard against him. His moan was short, deep, and utterly delicious.

It wasn't difficult to remember why she liked kissing him. He was so responsive, so willing to melt into her and take whatever she gave him. Her mind, the parts that weren't melting into the heat of the kiss, recalled yesterday's research. All things they'd need to talk about later. For now, she wanted to see just how far his responsiveness went.

She pushed at his hips, walking them backward until he fell on the bed and she landed on top of him, catching herself with her hands on either side of his shoulders, her legs straddling his hips. She broke the kiss and gave him a wicked look. "You ready for this?"

Noah was breathing heavily, his lips swollen and parted, his eyes alive with want. His words, though, told a different story. "Lucille," he said, not in the breathy, needy way she would have expected but in a let's-be-reasonable tone. His hands went to her hips and he gently pushed at her.

Lucille rolled off him and back to her feet. "What is it now, Noah?" she asked, crossing her arms, not caring what her robe was doing. If he didn't care about the skin she was revealing, why should she?

Noah sat up and crossed his legs. He looked rumpled and sexy and absolutely serious. "I think we should take things slower. I don't want to be some guy you fuck and then never talk to again."

"Noah," Lucille said in her best deadpan, "I have no illusions that you'd ever let that happen."

He frowned. "Is that a compliment or are you calling me a stalker?"

She shook her head. "I honestly don't know right now."

"Oh."

He was waiting. Waiting for her to say something, to share something about how he wouldn't be just a convenient body to have sex with and then move on. She didn't know what he was, but he wasn't that. For one thing, he irritated her too much to be convenient, for another, she didn't think one round of sex with Noah was going to do the trick. And, after yesterday, she was starting to think he was a good addition to the spin doctor team.

"If you're waiting for me to share my feelings, don't. I don't do that," Lucille said.

"I wasn't—"

"But," she continued, "I don't think this will be a one-off. I don't know what it is, but it's not casual. Does that work for you?"

Noah nodded. "Yeah, it does." Then he grinned. "So. This might be a good time to tell you that your left boob is hanging out."

Lucille glanced down. Sure enough, her robe had gaped open so her left breast was completely ex-posed. She hadn't felt it because of the heat still roaring through her body. The wicked smile re-turned to her face. "I see. Well, I am naked under this robe."

He gave a barely repressed groan.

"Do you want to see?" She met his gaze and had never felt so sexy in her life. Hell, she even twirled the tie on her robe.

"Yes," he breathed.

Lucille pulled on the tie. The silky robe fell to her feet, pooling on the floor and leaving her completely bare to him. She stalked forward, slower this time, and climbed onto the bed, straddling and rubbing against him.

"Noah?" she said, her voice a purr. She was enjoying this.

"Lucille?" he replied, his hands running gently up her thighs.

"I've noticed you seem turned on by me taking charge," she said, leaning in to murmur in his ear. She followed her words with a fierce tug on his earlobe that had him squirming under her. "Do you like it when I'm in charge?"

The *yes* Noah gasped out was such a sexy sound, she shivered. Damn, this man was pushing all her buttons.

"Do you like me right here, above you, pressing you into the bed? Controlling your pleasure?" she said as she kissed her way down his throat, pausing to suck on his neck. Not hard enough to leave a bruise, not this time. The way his skin shuddered under her lips was intoxicating. The way his body pushed up against her, hands grasping in the sheets as though he was trying to find something to ground him.

She paused and looked him in the face, wanting his honest answer. She might be new to a more openly dominant relationship, but she knew this type of thing required trust. Noah needed to trust her.

There was need in his eyes. An open eagerness to give her whatever she wanted. It was heady. "Yes. I want it."

Lucille slid a hand down to his straining erection and gave it a squeeze. "Good. Get these off and put your hands over your head."

"Are you going to restrain me?" he asked as she rolled off him again. His hands paused at the waistband of his underwear.

"Do you want that?"

Noah bit his lip again, but this time, it didn't seem to be deliberate. "At some point? But I don't think I'm ready for that yet."

Lucille smiled at him, a genuinely reassuring smile she hadn't used in a while. "Me neither. For now, let's see how well you follow directions."

The heat was back in Noah's gaze, but his hands hadn't moved. "Only in the bedroom though. I don't want to be ordered around all the time."

The smile turned into a smirk. "As if you'd let me." She paused and then answered honestly, "But yes, only in the bedroom."

Noah's body visibly relaxed, everywhere except the erection that seemed to strain harder again the black fabric. He finally followed her instructions and divested himself of the boxer briefs. With his gaze locked on hers, he slowly raised his arms over his head and clasped his hands.

"Do you have a condom?" he asked, his voice hoarse.

Lucille gave him a look. "Please. There are condoms everywhere in this house."

To illustrate her point, she reached into the pocket of her discarded robe and pulled out a foil packet. This she tossed on his chest before crawling up his body, slowly and intentionally. She ran her hands over his muscles, licking his lean brown chest and nipping him with her teeth. He watched her do it, not saying anything but letting her know he liked what was happening with little whimpers and desperate squirms, his hands twitching.

When they were face-to-face, Lucille kissed him. She licked his mouth. She bit his bottom lip. Her hands trailed lower, running over his abdomen and then lower still but never touching him where he wanted it most. When he bucked his hips, obviously looking for some kind of touch or friction, he pushed against her, rubbing her in a way that had her hurtling toward the edge faster than she thought possible.

"Lucille," Noah gasped, and the way he said her name was intoxicating. "I don't think I can hold on much longer."

The tension shimmered off his body. It matched the tension in her own. She gave a fierce, possessive growl into his neck that set him off even more. Lifting her head, she grabbed his searching erection and waited until he met her eyes to say, "Me neither. But next time. I'm taking my time with you."

She rolled the condom on as gracefully as she could manage and then sank down over it. They both groaned, and then Lucille started to move. Noah's hips rose to counter, and it was hard, fast, and messy. She rode Noah's body as he struggled not to move his hands, trying to get closer to her, pushing into her when she pulled back. They found their rhythm, she reached between them to appease her needy body, and that was it. Game over.

Lucille collapsed on Noah's chest for a few deep, gasping breaths. He unclasped his hands and started to wrap his arms around her, but she stopped him. She rolled off, disposed of the condom, then grabbed his left hand and started to massage it, pressing into the smooth skin of his palm to release any stiffness.

"What are you doing?" Noah asked even though it was obvious.

"Your hands were held together for a long time. You need to get the blood flow back." She sat next to him on the bed, naked and satisfied, her bare legs tucked under her. Noah lay flat on his back, his breathing returning to normal.

"You're taking care of me," he said.

Leave it to Noah to ruin the moment by explaining it. She sighed and dropped his hand. "Don't ruin this, Noah."

"Sorry," he said, looking disgruntled. "It's nice is all."

Christ. He was going to tell her he'd caught feelings next. The thought of which oddly didn't make her break out in hives. "I'm going to make coffee," she said. "Let me know when you're ready for round two."

Noah's reaction to her announcement was interrupted by the arrival of some unexpected, and, at the moment, unwelcome, guests.

CHAPTER SEVENTEEN

Brett awoke to the sun on his face. He squinted and blinked at the open curtains, trying to remember where he was. He lay in an extremely comfortable bed, far more comfortable than the bed at his apartment. Of course, that bed held the evidence of his slide back into sloven living. An empty bowl here, a hardbound copy of his favorite science fiction book there. Nothing compared to what it was before but not exactly the way he'd want to maintain a bed while cohabitating. And this comfortable bed that wasn't his was certainly cohabitated. There was an arm draped over his side, holding him against a hard, warm body.

Michel. The previous night sauntered back into his brain as it groggily woke up. Michel's burning kisses, their writhing bodies, the way he'd felt both scared and safe at the same time. Scared of the intensity of his feelings, the fervor of his connection with Michel, the all-encompassing passion. Yet, it was Michel, the man he'd known so well and now knew in a wholly different, physical way. The man he loved. But even as he thought it, he knew last night's sexual exploits didn't mark the moment he'd fallen in love with Michel, although they certainly had intensified the feeling. This might be the moment when he knew it, but he'd been in love with Michel for a long time.

The body behind him stirred and hot, soft lips pressed gently against the back of his neck. The lips traveled, exploring his neck and his hairline, meandering over to explore his ear. When that scorching mouth grabbed his earlobe between sharp teeth and gave a tug that shot through him on the border of pain and pleasure, Brett squirmed and rolled onto his back. He looked up to find Michel leaning over him, his gaze soft and sleepy, his mouth a satisfied smirk.

"Ouch," Brett said but smiled when he said it.

"What can I say," Michel said, smirking more, "I play hard."

With that, Michel dove into Brett's neck, sucking on his throat.

Brett was torn between staying utterly blissed out and pulling him up and onto his mouth. He allowed the neck sucking to go on for another few seconds and then tilted his head down to meet those curious, exploring lips. Michel gave up his pursuit of covering him with hickeys and went all-in on the kiss, plundering Brett's mouth again and again with his tongue, his hands running down his sides. It was all Brett could do to bury his fingers in Michel's hair and hold on for dear life.

Michel shifted so they were pressed together from the waist down. He began to move, and Brett rocked beneath him at the delicious sensation. When they were both panting and breathless, Michel broke away.

Brett whimpered and tried to pull him back. "No."

Michel pushed out of his reach and said gently, "Babe, I needed to get the lube."

If he wasn't so damn turned on, Brett might have found the statement hilarious, especially coming from his ultra-famous, serious boyfriend. But he was far too gone to acknowledge it and instead gave in to the sensations as Michel applied cool lube to both of their erections, rubbing them together until they came. Brett hadn't thought it was a real thing but he saw stars.

It was a long, breath-heaving, sweaty moment before he came down and back to the hotel room to find an equally panting and sweaty Michel slumped over him. He leaned in and kissed Michel's hair, smelling his shampoo and expensive styling products.

Michel grunted in response.

It wasn't until later, while they were still sitting naked in bed, post-shower, joined by a room service-provided breakfast, that reality crept back in. Michel brought it up first, taking a huge gulp of his coffee and then saying, "Brett. We need a new plan for dealing with your sisters."

Brett, his forkful of waffle halfway to his mouth, set it down regretfully and sighed. He couldn't look at Michel because Michel's body was naked and it was next to him and all of that meant it was a huge distraction. Michel's body did things to him, things he'd rather dwell on than discuss his siblings. "Yes, we do. I was thinking we should leave today. Avoiding them clearly doesn't work, and I don't want to risk another encounter."

Michel was quiet for what seemed like an eternity. "We can leave today. But we don't have to go right away. We can avoid them for a few more hours at least. But we're not going on another hike."

Brett laughed and couldn't resist ragging on his hiking aversion a little more. "Wait, don't you work out?"

Michel nodded. "But working out is vastly different than hiking. I've had about enough nature to last me the next ten years."

"Weren't you named an environmental icon last year?" Brett asked, still laughing.

Michel's face was serious as he said, "I care deeply about the environment, Brett. I just don't want to be out in it all the time."

Then he cracked a smile. "I don't think anyone on the nominating committee thought much of my speech. Although I have noticed that people don't seem to pay much attention when I talk." He frowned, contemplating the last bite of omelet on his plate. "Do you think they care more about how I look than what I say?"

Brett's eyebrows shot up. He couldn't believe what he was hearing. "You're just realizing this now? Michel, babe, you do know that half your fame is because you're hot, right?"

Michel gave him such a serious look that Brett's eyes widened. Did Michel really not know?

Then Michel broke out into delighted peals of laughter.

Brett smiled and buried his face in Michel's shoulder. It had been a while since he'd been so calm, so at ease, so at peace with who he was. It wasn't just the effects of great sex. At least he didn't think it was. The openness between them, the honesty, it felt like they were in a magical bubble where nothing in the outside world mattered any longer. Not sisters, not labels, not anything.

"Brett," Michel said, "I think you make me a funnier person."

Brett straightened so he could give Michel a look. "What?"

"It's true," Michel said, cutting a sausage with his knife and fork. "I've never been thought of as funny before and here I am, having hilarious thoughts about sausages and making jokes about my appearance."

Brett laughed. "What kinds of thoughts about sausages?"

Michel stopped cutting, stabbed a piece of said sausage with his fork, brought it to his mouth, and ate it, staring into Brett's eyes the whole time. He swallowed.

Brett nearly came on the sheets. "Jesus, Michel. If you keep doing that, I will jump you and ravish you."

"Promises, promises."

Brett contemplated the breakfast spread out on the bed. He wondered what would be the easiest, no fastest, way to clear it.

A knock on the room door interrupted this devious line of thinking.

"The mimosas," Michel said.

"I'd go get them, but…" Brett said, hoping Michel got the hint he was rocking an erection and wouldn't be answering any doors at the moment.

Michel slid out from under the sheets, throwing him a wicked grin. Brett had a moment to enjoy the sight of naked Michel before he put on one of the hotel bathrobes and left the room.

Brett heard Michel talking to someone and then the door closed. He waited, eating his waffle. It should have taken Michel all of ten seconds to get back to the room, glasses of booze in hand. Instead, he waited.

"Michel?" he called. "Everything okay?"

Having a boyfriend who tended to get in life-threatening scrapes wasn't making this an easy moment for Brett. His bubble of tranquility popped long before Michel returned to the bedroom. Popped by fears of the person at the door not being room services with drinks but someone who was inexplicably pissed at Michel for some reason and wanted to kidnap him. Might it be someone from the crime club? That woman Danielle who'd thought Simon and Michel were an item and had tried to destroy him to get to Simon? Or another member of the club who hadn't taken well to Michel's interruption or how he'd led the media to them and broken up their secret meeting? These were very real, and very dangerous, possibilities.

When Michel did return, he wasn't holding any glasses of orange juice and champagne. He was holding his phone. The phone Michel probably hadn't checked since the day before.

"Oh, thank God," Brett began, "I thought someone had—"

Michel cut him off. "Sylvia's out of rehab?"

Brett, in his relief Michel wasn't kidnapped, forgot all about not telling him about Sylvia. To be honest, he'd forgotten all about Sylvia. "Oh, that. Yeah, Lucille texted me about it two days ago."

"But you didn't tell me?"

The broken moment was squashed into the obscenely expensive carpeting.

CHAPTER EIGHTEEN

"Lucy? Are you home?"

Lucille barely had time to react when the sound of Simon's voice reached her. "Seriously?" She grabbed her robe and held it closed over her body.

"Does your uncle have a key to your house?" Noah asked. Lucille was glad he wasn't still spread out naked on the bed and was throwing on clothes.

"Apparently." She grimaced. "I didn't give him one."

"Lucy?" Simon's voice grew closer and they both stared in horror at the open bedroom door. There'd been no reason to close it, not when the apartment was empty.

"Simon," she said as she stalked out of the room, pulling her robe tighter and putting on her most ferocious glare. "What the fuck?"

Simon stood in the main room of the condo, and he wasn't alone. He had JP with him. While JP would probably be her uncle-in-law someday and while they'd been to a fake orgy together, Lucille didn't think JP was at all prepared to see her post-sex, in nothing but a short bathrobe. He was looking with determined fascination at everything not Lucille.

Simon was dressed in what he termed vacation fancy. Tight, salmon-colored capris, a tucked-in pale-blue shirt, and huge white sunglasses. JP, meanwhile, wore the usual jeans and nerdy t-shirt he always did when he didn't have to dress up.

"Lucy," Simon exclaimed, "what are you wearing? And what is going on with your hair?"

Dammit. She had sex hair. "I think the more pressing question is when did you get a key to my house?"

"Is that really important right now? More important than, say, why you just came out of the guest room?" Simon gave her a look that meant he knew exactly what she was up to and wasn't going to let it go until she confessed.

"Simon." JP spoke up. "I thought you were going to start asking people if you could have keys to their house."

"Was I?"

Lucille rolled her eyes. "Hi, JP. Sorry to rush out here not dressed and everything. I didn't want Simon to come barging in."

JP nodded. "Understandable."

Simon leaned over to his boyfriend and said in a loud whisper, "Because she's got a naked man in there."

Lucille gave Simon her coldest glare. "Make yourselves at home. I'm going to go find some clothes."

Back in the hall, she ran into Noah. "Fix your damn hair," she hissed at him.

He looked her up and down. "Uh, if you went out there looking like that, I really don't think my hairstyle matters."

Lucille glared at him until he ducked around her and out into the main room. She slipped into her bedroom and locked the door. She allowed herself to slump against it for a few seconds. What a morning. An hour ago, she'd been lying in bed contemplating all the work she needed to get done. Then she'd fucked Noah, which had been a surprise. Not the sex itself. They were two attractive, hetero-leaning single people with an incredible amount of tension between them. Having sex was inevitable. What had been surprising was how much she'd enjoyed it, how much she enjoyed Noah. And had she really told him it wasn't something casual? She had.

Contemplation time was over. Yes, Simon had once again interrupted her first sexy times with a new fling, but Simon didn't show up without a purpose. He appeared in her living room when he wanted something from her or wanted her to do something. Or had something to say that he didn't want to tell her over the phone. JP's presence, though, was more of a puzzle. Apart from their adventure at the not-sex party, JP wasn't one for spontaneous travel.

She chose one of her power outfits, a bold yellow jumpsuit with wide, stiff legs, a halter-neck top, and a deep, revealing back. She put a white suit jacket over the top to complete the look. Then there was her hair. There wasn't time for her to do much more with it than run a brush through and pull it back into a high ponytail. She applied a quick layer of makeup and strutted out of her room looking ready to kick ass and take names.

In the living room, the men had taken her at her word and looked comfortable indeed. Or, at least, Noah and Simon did. JP looked concerned, his brow furrowed and his leg bouncing in place.

She ignored Noah's reaction to her, his eyebrows raised in appreciation. She hadn't put this on for his benefit, although she couldn't say it wasn't a nice bonus.

"Talk," she said to her uncle, crossing her arms and glaring. "Although, if this has anything to do with me becoming friends with Sylvia Stanton, did you really need to come all this way to gloat? And drag poor JP along?"

Her uncle snorted. "Please, Lucy. You know I absolutely would come all this way to gloat. But that's not why I'm here."

"Is that right?"

"It is right. JP?"

JP, still looking worried, spoke. "I was able to trace the call. And I'm going to save my lecture about how I'm not your personal phone tracer and how highly illegal it is to use my company for this kind of stuff whenever you want. Because I think we actually have a problem."

Lucille had forgotten about the phone trace. She'd been a little busy fighting and fucking Noah. But now she remembered. Brett. The weird text and weirder way his sisters had known where to find him.

"Who was it?" Noah jumped in. He leaned forward on the couch, watching JP, but, Lucille noticed, still angling his body toward her. If she had to guess, she'd say he was equally disappointed they hadn't gotten to round two.

"The phone belongs to a Lauren Cunningham," JP said.

"Lauren Cunningham?" The name was familiar in a vague way. Like the woman had once been a someone and when she no longer was, Lucille forgot all about her.

"Formerly Lauren Fontile of the Fontile Agency?" Simon added.

Lucille locked eyes with him and his expression, or lack of expression, told her nothing. Lauren Fontile, she remembered. Of course, she remembered her. The woman had been a big deal—she'd represented dozens of big-name actors and screenwriters. She was known for swooping in on the rising stars and getting them to sign with her before anyone had even heard of them. And two months later, that rising star was everywhere.

"Who's that?" Noah asked.

"She was a highly successful agent a few years ago. One of the most sought-after agents in the business. But no one's heard from her since she mysteriously closed her agency and disappeared," Lucille explained. She sat in one of the plush armchairs that framed the couch, suspecting this conversation was going to take a while.

"Brett didn't tell you?" Simon had on one of his snide looks. The one he often wore when talking to or about Brett. And here Lucille thought Simon liked

Brett better now he wasn't dating her. Of course, he was now dating their friend and most profitable client, so it seemed Simon's animosity had merely been refocused.

"We didn't spend much time talking—"

Simon's snort was louder this time.

"—about his screenwriting career."

She didn't look at Noah. Why should she? What happened between her and Brett had nothing to do with him. Although, after Simon's implications, she couldn't help wondering if he was jealous.

"He told me," JP said.

Both Antons turned to him simultaneously.

"What? When?" Simon demanded.

Lucille just raised her eyebrows. She wasn't surprised Brett would confide something in JP. Of the people in the room, JP was the most trustworthy, certainly the most honest of all of them and the one least likely to sell someone's secrets for money.

"Brett and I talk," said JP with a shrug. "We're friends."

Judging by Simon's expression, this wasn't a possibility he was prepared for, nor one he particularly liked.

"What do you have against Brett?" Noah asked.

"We don't have time to go into it," Simon said.

"Meaning, he doesn't know," Lucille said.

"We're getting off topic. Can we focus, please?" Simon glared around at all of them, including his boyfriend. "Lauren Fontile was Brett's agent for *Night Before the Apocalypse*. The moment Brett got the offer from Stanton, she swooped in and snatched him up, signing him for a three-film contract. When Brett didn't deliver the second script, Lou Stanton got nasty. There were rumors he didn't want to do anything to sour the family relationship, so he blacklisted Lauren Fontile instead."

Lucille frowned. "Why didn't I hear about this?"

"Lou Stanton had it covered up well. Poured cement over the whole thing and Lauren's career."

"How did you hear about it?" Lucille didn't like it when Simon knew something she didn't. It was the basis of their relationship, keeping secrets from each other, but this was a big one about *her* ex-boyfriend.

Simon shot a glance at JP before he said, "I was hooking up with one of Lou Stanton's lawyers at the time. The guy was on vacation and ended up being one of my more profitable marks."

If JP had thoughts about Simon's fugitive exploits, he didn't say so. Instead, he said, "That's not right. It was the story Lou told the people he needed to, but Brett told me the truth. Lou fired him first. He didn't give a fuck about their familial relationship. But, around the same time, Lou discovered Lauren Fontile had been embezzling money from him for years and he used the broken contract with Brett to cover up his embarrassment."

"So now Lauren's pissed at Brett for getting her caught and, what? She sent his sisters to sabotage his new relationship?" Noah said. "Sounds pretty weak to me."

"Lauren Fontile was embezzling from Lou Stanton," Simon mused, clearly taken with the idea.

"No, she's up to something more than that." Lucille stood. "No one goes to so much trouble to embarrass the person who destroyed their career."

She looked at Simon. This time, Simon's expression told her everything.

"Yes," he said, "I agree. It's too much work for so little reward. The sisters would do their thing, but as a prelude, a first step toward...what?"

"That's what I need to find out." Lucille left the room. She went into her bedroom, straight to the closet, and got down her small, rolling carry-on bag. It would be a quick trip, but she wasn't about to show up unprepared. Especially if she somehow ended up in the hospital again and everyone else was at the police station and couldn't bring her a change of clothes. Being in that situation once had been enough.

"Lucille."

She eyed the two dresses in front of her. They were both beach dresses in tropical prints, perfect for blending in poolside or at a tiki bar. The question remained, what color was everyone wearing to the beach and the tiki bars these days? Which one would blend in better? She'd have to take both.

She turned to find Noah behind her.

He stood in her closet doorway, frowning. He still had sex hair and she wanted to both straighten it and mess it up even more. "What are you doing?"

"Packing," she said simply because it was obvious.

"You're not going to the island, are you?"

"Of course, I am." She decided on platform sandals with triangle cutouts in the heels. Her feet looked amazing in them.

"Why?"

"Why?" she echoed, not understanding what he wasn't understanding. "Because my friend is in trouble."

"You don't know that." He seemed upset, angry even. For no reason. "All we know is Brett's sisters showed up at the same hotel at the same time as him and that this Lauren woman sent him a cryptic text. There's no evidence to support your conclusions."

"Noah." Her exasperation rose. She didn't have time to stand around arguing with him. And this was swiftly becoming an argument. "I know Brett and Michel. I know people like Lauren. Fuck, you do, too. Can you imagine if you'd stood around waiting for more evidence when Danielle held Michel and Simon at gunpoint?"

"It's not even close to the same situation. I'd been undercover with Danielle for months. You hardly knew anything about this Lauren person until three minutes ago."

"I know her career was destroyed, and I can make a damn good guess she blames Brett for it. Do you think she'd settle for calling in his family to embarrass him in front of Michel? Because I don't."

"So, you're going to rush off to a tropical island on the off-chance Brett and Michel are in trouble?" His voice was harsh.

"Yes."

"Is one of the celebrity spin doctor services you offer? How much does a service like that run for?" The harshness transformed into biting sarcasm. He folded his arms, his jaw clenched.

Lucille continued packing during his outburst. She zipped her suitcase, stood, and walked past him, pulling the carry-on behind her. "Are you done with your little tantrum or are you going to keep being a dick?"

Noah's dark eyes narrowed as he fumed at her. If he was waiting for her to crack, to show he upset her or that she'd listen to him, he was going to be waiting a long time. "I'm coming with you," he said finally.

"Fine. But if you keep being an ass, I will throw you out of the plane. Speaking of which..."

Lucille popped her head around the doorway to the living room. Simon and JP were sitting close together, appearing to talk to each other. Lucille called bullshit. They'd been listening to her and Noah fight and probably had a bet on who would win. "How'd you get here?"

"We finally sprang for a corporate jet," JP said.

"That's what I was hoping you'd say. Mind if we borrow it?"

Chapter Nineteen

I t took Brett a few minutes to realize Michel was actually upset. It took even less time for all the anxiety and crushing inadequacy to come flooding back. For a brief few hours, the negative thoughts had been quiet, drowned out by a tidal wave of positive emotion. Now, in their return, he noticed their absence. He didn't know why the thoughts were back, but they were, chanting *not good enough* loudly in his head.

He sat on the bed, the breakfast tray on his lap, opening and closing his mouth like a fish.

"Brett." Michel's tone was questioning and something else. Annoyed? Or hurt? He stood in the doorway, his bathrobe tied tightly around his sculpted body, his perfect features crumpled. "Why didn't you tell me Sylvia was out of rehab?"

Part of Brett wondered why it mattered where Sylvia was and what she was doing. But a bigger part of him knew it mattered to Michel and he hated that. "Lucille texted me and I didn't think about it after that."

Michel's frown deepened.

He told the truth, and yet, it sounded like a lie. He hadn't thought about keeping the news from Michel, not consciously. But he'd known, when he read the text, there was no way he'd be sharing the information until he had to.

"There has been a lot going on...but this is the woman who tried to kill me on multiple occasions. The woman I anguished over for years, who I lived in fear of for months, the woman who almost killed *us*. You didn't think it was important for me to know she's back?"

Michel was being dramatic. Or was he? Brett hadn't seen much of him during the years he'd been with Sylvia, and they'd never talked about it. It was true Sylvia had tried to kill them. He'd been around for it, and his shoulder ached at the memory. "Okay, so yeah, I should have told you. I don't know, there were...other things on my mind."

Michel shook his head. "No. It's not like you. It doesn't make sense that you wouldn't tell me. You who know what Sylvia is like and what she's capable of."

Brett waited for more, but Michel seemed to be thinking. He moved the breakfast tray off his lap and left the bed, heading for his suitcase and some clean clothes. He got as far as putting his pants on, his shirt still over his head, when Michel started asking questions.

"Have you heard anything else? Where she is? What she's doing?"

He pulled his shirt down harder than he meant to. He needed to see Michel's expression. But Michel's features were closed off, so he was forced to ask. "Why do you want to know?"

The words came out harsh.

Michel frowned again. "What else are you keeping from me, Brett?"

Brett clenched his jaw and when he spoke, there was anger in his voice. "Nothing. I'm not keeping anything from you."

"Are you sure about that?"

He didn't mean to lose his temper. He didn't know why he did. Maybe it was the pent-up anxiety, the stress of his sisters being nearby. And he couldn't understand why Michel needed to know about Sylvia, nor why it was bothering him so much. "I'm not keeping anything from you. I have no fucking clue where Sylvia is, but I'm guessing she's in

LA. Good thing we're leaving today, huh? Not long to wait before your reunion."

When Michel didn't respond, Brett glared at him. Michel was staring at him like he'd never seen Brett before. "You think I want to see Sylvia? Is that why you didn't tell me about her? Because you think I'll jump at the chance to get back together with her?"

Michel's words hurt. They hit his skin and burrowed in.

Brett needed space. The bedroom was closing in on him, constricting and claustrophobic. He pushed past Michel, careful not to touch him, and into the living room. Better. Momentarily. Then he heard Michel behind him, following him.

He stared at the couch. The couch where they'd made out two days and an eternity ago. He needed to be honest. He needed to come clean, to expose his soft underbelly and see what Michel did with it. But the last time he'd exposed his soft underbelly to Michel, when he'd done it without even intending to, he'd lost Michel and spent the next two years in a drunken haze of regret and misery.

It was right after Brett sold the rights for *The Night Before the Apocalypse* to his uncle. Right after Michel had met Sylvia Stanton and was, by all accounts, smitten with her. It was the night Michel told Brett he and Sylvia were buying a house together, moving out of the city and into the gated communities of the suburbs. Brett hadn't wanted Michel to go. He told him he didn't think Sylvia was a good match, that it was too soon for him to know what Sylvia was really like. Michel didn't believe him, grew angry, and they'd parted, not to see each other again until the night of the premiere when Michel told him about Sylvia's murderous tendencies.

At the time, Brett hadn't known he was putting his heart on his line. It would take him those couple of years to realize the full extent of his feelings for Michel. But he did know he was desperate not to lose his best friend. He knew he'd tried to tell Michel the truth about Sylvia, tried to tell him why he shouldn't be with her. But Michel hadn't believed him and had left anyway.

"I didn't even consider telling you. I didn't want to because..." Brett swallowed.

"Yes?"

Michel's voice, normally his favorite sound in the world, cut into him. He turned to face the man he knew with absolute certainty he loved. "I don't know, Michel. I think I was jealous. I...I can't see why you'd want to be with me when Sylvia is available again."

"Sylvia, who tried to murder me."

Brett nodded.

Michel sighed. He didn't sound angry, he sounded exasperated. "You're a fucking idiot, Brett."

Brett glanced up at him, hopefully. Michel had his head tilted back, the long line of his neck exposed in the robe. Brett wanted to lick it. He wanted to close the distance between them, jump on Michel, and head back into the haven of their bed. Maybe they could return to the moment before Michel left to get the drinks. This time, Brett would get them or they'd say fuck the drinks, we don't need them anyway. This time, they wouldn't leave the bed, Michel wouldn't look at his phone, and this argument wouldn't start.

Then Michel spoke. "Brett. I get it. I've met your family, who are horrible. I see why you have this inferiority complex. I get it. You think I'm completely stable all the time? Have you seen *Mountaintop*?"

In the film, Michel played a man who sat on top of a mountain for five years, refusing to talk to anyone, until his best friend returned and apologized to him. The film had won Michel six acting awards and had briefly caused him to lose his hold on reality.

Brett smiled weakly. "So, you're not breaking up with me?"

He immediately wished he could take the words back. How needy and desperate did he sound? What if Michel hadn't thought about breaking up, but now did because Brett introduced the subject?

Michel lowered his head. He met Brett's gaze. His face was serious, a game face he used for his dramatic roles, the award-winning ones. His eyes were unreadable. Brett wanted to think he looked forgiving, but he knew it wouldn't hold up in court.

"You don't trust me, Brett," Michel said carefully.

It was Brett's turn to explode. "What do you mean I don't trust you? I followed you to an island to help you rescue my murderous cousin. I followed you to a meeting of a very dangerous celebrity crime club. What do you mean I don't trust you?"

He failed to mention he'd been unconscious when he was put on the flight to the island and he'd gone to the club because he was sick with worry over what trouble Michel had gotten himself into. He wouldn't mention those details, not if he wanted Michel to believe him. He did trust Michel, didn't he?

Michel shook his head. "No, you don't trust me to take care of myself. None of you do. Lucille, Simon... I expect them not to trust me to make my own decisions. That's what I pay them for. But you? You didn't even trust me enough to tell me you were nervous about us having sex."

Brett froze. "You...you knew about that?"

"Of course, I knew. It would have taken a monumentally unobservant person to miss how you panicked every time we began to get intimate."

"Oh." Brett didn't know what else to say. He didn't know what he felt anymore. Numb. Sad. Terrified that this was the end of the best thing that had ever happened to him and it was all his fault.

"It's okay, Brett. It's not a big deal. I think most people are nervous their first time with someone they care about."

Michel's words washed over him. He'd been staring at the floor again and forced himself to return to Michel's face. "Does this mean we're okay?" he asked, carefully.

Michel looked at him, his expression one of great sadness and Brett knew before Michel spoke. "No. It doesn't mean we're okay."

"So, what does that mean?" Brett squeaked, his voice hoarse.

"Just...give me some time."

Brett's panic rose. He couldn't stay in the room. The room that had been so full of happiness until he'd ruined it. He turned, a rushing sound in his ears, and bolted out the door. His phone buzzed in his pocket, but he knew it wasn't Michel, so it didn't matter.

Chapter Twenty

"Why don't we have a private plane?"

Lucille looked up from her tablet as Noah's question broke their icy silence. They had successfully borrowed JP's company jet with the promise they wouldn't get it blown up and would return it the following day. It'd taken some convincing to secure the plane. Normally, it was JP who protested the use of his company property for their spin doctor-related exploits, but JP had an empathy loophole wherein, if one of his friends was in trouble, he would do whatever he could to help. Simon, however, was not thrilled about them taking the jet. His argument was, "Is saving Brett really worth it?"

At which point, Lucille reminded him Michel was also on the island and potentially in danger, and did Simon want to risk his most profitable client? Again? Simon grumbled but, in the end, agreed to fly commercial on the way home.

Lucille texted Brett to let him know they were coming and to stay put. He wouldn't listen, but she had to try. She hoped they arrived before Lauren Cunningham, or whatever she was calling herself now, put her final plan into action. He didn't reply.

"They're too conspicuous," Lucille said in response to Noah's question.

Noah nodded and looked out the window at the fluffy clouds and brilliant afternoon sun. Sometime in between fighting with her and their quick departure, Noah had had time to do his hair and change into a gray suit and bright yellow shirt. He looked completely put-together—professional, stylish, and, although Lucille would never tell him this, she was impressed with how he perfectly matched her in both boldness of clothing choice and composure. She didn't need his head getting more inflated than it was. Besides, she was mad at him.

She tore her eyes away from him and returned to her email. She hadn't been exaggerating when she'd woken him up a few hours ago and said they had an enormous amount of work waiting. Her inbox was bursting, and it didn't seem like Noah was going to be much help, obsessed as he was with ogling the private jet.

It was a nice jet. Not as large as Michel's, but there was enough space for eight people to fly in complete comfort. The décor was less ostentatious than Michel's plane. Instead of velvet and black leather, everything in the LT Tech jet was a sleek silver, designed like one of their devices to be a piece of utter technological beauty. Lucille could understand Noah's distraction. She herself considered running off with the thing and sending JP an IOU in the mail.

The first ten emails were from Christy-Anne, who hadn't contacted her in months. Lucille skipped over those, undecided if she'd even read them, and moved on to the eleventh, one from Sylvia. Odd how much difference a day and a really good lunch meeting could make. She opened the email, excited to hear from the heiress for the first time ever.

Luce,

The producer called me already. This reality show is happening and it's happening now. I, of course, have a completely incompetent production team and already had to fire my stylist for suggesting leopard print. Can you even?

Send me the name of that stylist you know, would you? I need someone who wouldn't be caught dead in animal print. Obviously, this show is going to be a complete shit fest. That's what people want to see. But

I should be able to look good while doing it. Is that too much to ask? Apparently for some of these fuckers, it is.

How are things with Noah the hottie? He may be a complete tool, but he's gotta be good for some fun.

Lunch next week? Not brunch. Brunch is for losers.
Sylvia

Lucille grinned as she read the email and shot back a reply with her stylist's number and a suggested lunch date. It was rare to find someone who shared her opinion on brunch and further proof that, whatever else came out of this mess, Sylvia was a keeper.

"What are you smiling about?"

Her grin disappeared and she gave Noah a slowly simmering look of annoyance. "Are you going to do any work or are you going to sit and stare at me?"

He returned her glare with a suggestive waggle of his eyebrows. "I don't know. Depends on what you're up for. A quickie in the bathroom? Some heavy petting right out here in the main cabin?"

Lucille's body, still upset their second round had been interrupted that morning, perked up. "Neither," she said. "I, unlike some people, am working tirelessly to provide the best service to our clients."

"Is that why you're ignoring Christy-Anne's emails and emailing Sylvia Stanton about lunch?"

This really annoyed her. "How the hell can you see my screen? You're on the other side of the aisle."

Noah had tried to sit across from her when they'd first gotten on the plane, but she'd given him a death glare and he'd, wisely for once, taken a seat diagonally from her.

"The angle you're holding your tablet to keep the screen from me means it's perfectly reflected in the window," he said, his voice smug.

God, he was annoying. A deeply sexy, competent type of annoying.

"So, you took it as an invitation to read my emails?" she asked, inflecting her tone with haughtiness.

"I assumed, since you've made such a big deal about working, your *work*-related emails wouldn't be private from your *coworker*." He crossed one leg over the other knee and stretched back into his seat, his whole demeanor a picture of innocent bullshit.

Don't play that game with me. I invented that game. "You want to see what my work emails are like? Do you?"

He flashed her a brief frown. He didn't seem sure what she was up to. It was how she liked him best. "Okay. Yes. Sure."

Lucille cleared her throat dramatically and tapped on the first of Christy-Anne's messages, the subject line reading *Did you fucking block me.* "L. Did you change your number and not fucking tell me? I hate email. I fucking pay you to answer your phone. What the shit," Lucille read aloud. "Message number two says 'Seriously L? It's been ten fucking minutes. Call me back. My agent won't answer my calls. I tried to make a goddamn friend, but it didn't work and I need you to do some cover up. My so-called fucking friend filmed a video of me and now is threatening to leak it and did I mention my agent won't take my calls? What the hell am I supposed to do with that?'"

"Jesus," Noah said in a low whistle.

"The rest are just a lot of swearing and increasingly personal insults," Lucille said, scrolling through the other eight messages. "No wait, in the last one she decides it's not worth talking to me after all and fires me. I guess I'll have to call her when we get back."

"I take it she's profitable?"

"Like you wouldn't believe. Although I distinctly remember telling her to lose my number for her own good. I guess it didn't take," Lucille said with a shrug. Some of her clients were like that. The same cycle over and over again. Personally, if she were stuck in something so self-destructive, she hoped someone in her life would force her to break out of it. Simon? Not likely. Brett? Maybe, if he could get out of his own destruction. Possible JP or Michel. Noah? He didn't seem like a guy who would stand silently by while she spiraled out of control. As mad as she was at him, she had to admit he'd been the only one to question her about once again rushing off to rescue Brett and Michel.

"I could do it."

Lucille pulled herself out of her reverie. Just in time too, since those thoughts were making her feel things. Things that were warm and fuzzy and not at all the fiery rage and cold exterior she was trying to maintain. "You could do what?"

"Call Christy-Anne back. Take her on as a client." He shrugged and typed something into his laptop.

Lucille considered it. On one hand, she didn't want to seem like she needed the help. She didn't. She'd been dealing with Christy-Anne for years and could handle her. On the other hand, not dealing with Christy-Anne anymore would be a dream come true. It would free up her time to take on the less profitable but far more interesting clients. "Think you're up to it?"

Noah laughed. "I've been hanging around you, haven't I? How hard can managing one nutty celebrity be?"

She bristled. "Don't you dare compare me to Christy-Anne."

He stopped laughing and looked surprised. "I wasn't. I meant you are the queen, no, the empress of delivering crushing blows without a word. Working with someone like Christy-Anne will be a walk in the park."

She narrowed her eyes. Noah's words were causing the warmth to spread. He thought she was the master of the crushing look. Which meant he'd been crushed by her. Which meant he had some feelings for her, some emotions to be crushed. Interesting. No one had ever paid her such a high compliment.

She didn't tell him that. "Since you seem determined to have a productivity comparison, what have you been working on besides staring around wide-eyed?"

She was prepared for Noah to look chastised. She was prepared for him to argue or try to explain himself. She wasn't prepared for him to cross the aisle in a quick step and slide into the seat next to her. She didn't even have time to reflexively move away from him, leaving their arms pressed together on the shared armrest.

Noah looked down at his laptop, his face turned from hers, not appearing to notice how much touching they were doing. "I've been doing some research on Lauren Cunningham, which is the name she's still going by, if the hotel registry is correct."

"You hacked into the hotel registry?" Lucille asked, impressed.

He shook his head. "No, JP did. Have you noticed the man's moral code basically goes out the window when his friends are in trouble?"

"Yes, it's one of the great things about JP."

Noah smiled. "I found an article about Stanton Enterprises dropping Brett and the cancelation of the second movie in the series, but it doesn't mention his agent. Then there's this other article that includes a statement from Lauren Fontile, but it's a generic spin, nothing there. The embezzlement scandal was buried and buried deep."

Lucille found herself examining Noah's profile. He had a great profile, his features smooth and beautifully proportioned, all the way down to the dark scruffiness of his unshaven chin. He wouldn't have forgotten to shave, not when his hair was swooped to perfection. So, he'd left the scruff there intentionally, perhaps to add a little roguishness to his appearance?

Whatever his reason, it was working, damn him.

"After Brett's contract ended, she mostly disappeared. She popped up here and there in society pages, always as an unknown engaged to someone rich and famous. She seems to have gone through a few husbands before the late Lord Cunningham."

"Nothing about what happened to her husbands?" Lucille asked. She had to admit, she was intrigued. Not so much about Lauren Cunningham going after Brett, but about the woman herself.

"Nothing."

Before she could stop herself, she said, "You're good at this."

He turned his head, frowning, his face close to hers. "At researching? I hope so. I was a PI for years and both my parents are teachers."

"I meant the whole celebrity spin doctor job. You're good at it."

A smile replaced his frown. "Was that a compliment?"

Lucille rolled her eyes. Then she pressed her lips together, not to keep herself from kissing him, but to keep herself from asking more questions, from showing interest in his life. But...she wanted to know. She wanted to be interested. "How did you go from a house full of teachers to being a private investigator?"

He chuckled. "Kinda weird, huh? I'd like to say it's a long story, but it's not. I didn't want to teach, dropped out of college, ran into this PI on a case, and convinced him to teach me the ropes. That's about it. As it turned out, I was good at finding dirt on people."

She wanted to tell him how shitty his storytelling was and how his casual recitation had raised so many more questions than it answered. But she didn't get the chance to say anything as the plane chose that moment to land on Reef Island.

A few minutes later, Lucille strolled into the resort lobby, wearing huge white sunglasses and a large hat, followed by Noah. Another thing JP had found for them was Michel and Brett's room number. They also knew Lauren Cunningham's room, but Lucille wanted to assure herself her friends were safe before taking on Brett's nemesis.

A decidedly dejected Michel in a hotel bathrobe opened the door when they knocked. "Lucille? Noah? What are you doing here?"

"I texted Brett to tell you we were coming," Lucille said, impatient to get on with the more pressing questions—where was the former Lady Cunningham at that moment and what was she up to.

Michel stepped back from the door and let them in. "Brett doesn't tell me anything anymore," Michel said, his voice heartbreakingly sad. His appearance, normally so groomed, was disheveled in a gorgeous way. It was the thing about Michel. Even when he was trying not to care how he looked, he looked amazing.

"What do you mean Brett doesn't tell you anything?" Noah asked, going on to ask the question Lucille didn't know if she could bring herself to say aloud. "He's not...dead, is he?"

This snapped Michel out of his melancholic state. "What? No, Brett's not dead. Why would he be dead?"

"Because there's someone on this island, his former agent actually, who wants revenge on him. She brought his sisters here and we have no idea what she'll do next," Lucille said, her voice as clear and steady as she could make it.

Michel's face constricted even more. "Another thing Brett kept from me."

Lucille wanted to roll her eyes. Beside her, she heard Noah let out a long, exasperated sigh. She understood the sentiment. When Michel got going, he gave it his all. A juvenile part of her brain made a sex joke out of it. She ignored it. "And you can tell him that later. Right now, we need calm and collected Michel, okay? Not sad-bathrobe-wearing Michel. You do care about Brett, don't you? Even though you seem to be on the outs?"

"Of course, I do. I love Brett," said Michel with all the passion of an award acceptance speech.

"Good. Now get dressed. We have to find him before she does."

Two minutes later, they were out the door, jogging down the hallway, with no idea where Brett might be.

Chapter Twenty-One

The bar was a fish tank, topped with glass so drinkers could watch the occupants while enjoying their overpriced cocktails.

Brett sat at a high-top table in the corner of the resort bar and restaurant, trying not to wax poetically about the sorry state of his affairs and doing so anyway. It was Michel who brought out this side of him, he decided. Michel and his stupid handsome face and amazing body and how much he just fucking cared. Michel cared about him. Hell, Michel cared about him more than he cared about himself most of the time. For God knew what reason, Michel loved him. In spite of his awful family and personal failures and sexual inexperience, Michel loved him. Instead of trusting that love, learning from his mistakes, and being open with Michel, he'd screwed everything up.

His words kept echoing back to him. He wasn't jealous of Sylvia, not really. He didn't think Michel was going to leave him for her. Or, rather, his rational faculties didn't think so. His anxiety, the force that'd run riot back in the room, certainly thought so. Its poison remained, aching through his body, filling him with deep, abysmal despair.

He didn't even know where to begin to apologize to Michel. Should he even try right now when Michel had told him, in no uncertain terms, he needed space and lots of it?

The ice cubes in his glass clinked as he tightened his grip so much his hand shook with the effort. The liquid in the glass, soda water with lime, was long since gone. Brett contemplated ordering another and this time adding whiskey to the mix. But no, he wasn't going to backslide completely.

It was early afternoon, and the bar and restaurant hadn't begun to fill for lunch. A few small groups of guests enjoyed a late breakfast. Outside, the weather was tropical island perfect—sunny, warm, a slight breeze nudging the huge, brightly colored flowers to release their perfume into the air. A sultry day. A day of promise.

A few hours ago, still tangled in the sheets with Michel, Brett would have loved this day. Now he hated it. Was it too much to ask for dark clouds and rain to match his dark mood?

He was so busy glaring at the scene outside the window he didn't notice his sisters' approach until they were at his table. When he did notice them, he immediately wished he hadn't. He glared out the window even more fervently, hoping they'd take the hint and go the fuck away.

"Brett," Evelyn said, smacking the table with her hand and leaning in so he couldn't avoid looking at her.

Brett instinctively leaned back, remembered he was sitting on a stool, and caught himself with some abdominal muscles he didn't know he had. "Evelyn," he said, matching her intensity, in tone at least.

Few could match her intensity in outfits. She wore a loose, shimmery silver shirt that gleamed in the light of the tropical afternoon, a tight lemon-yellow mini skirt, and tall platform sandals with clear heels that lit up when she walked.

Patience stood behind her wearing all black.

"We're leaving," Evelyn said like she was stating the very obvious.

Brett looked down to the floor and saw their luggage, piled high and ready to roll. "Okay," he said, not wanting to have this conversation nor understanding why they'd bother to seek him out to say goodbye. Last night, they'd been ready to disown him for hiding Michel. "Have a safe trip home," he said, just to have something to say.

Evelyn rolled her eyes at him. "We wanted to tell you we understand why you didn't tell us you're dating Michel."

Brett was really caught off guard at that. "Oh," he said.

"Yes," Patience added. "It will be difficult and embarrassing for you to explain to the family when he breaks up with you. First, you're giving Evie and Mom this incredible access to their idol, and then you lose it for them when you inevitably fuck up the relationship. It makes sense you wouldn't want to explain to them why you're not good enough for him."

And there it was. But, in the haze of his own pain and misery, their barbs failed to hit their mark. Patience's extreme, blunt carelessness and the way Evelyn was looking at him like she pitied his sad life rolled off him. Normally, he'd pretend not to be hurt, but secretly his heart would break a little more. But he'd already screwed up with Michel and, compared to that, what else mattered? What did it matter if his family was filled with horrible self-centered people?

He had his own family, his own people he could count on.

Later, maybe these thoughts would energize him into action. For now, he was too heartbroken to do more than stare blankly at his sisters. "Sure, that's it," he said with deadpan sarcasm.

Evelyn nodded. "I thought so. It's okay, Brett. We're still your family, even if you are a complete fuckup."

Brett didn't bother listening. "What about the things Michel said to you?" he asked. He wanted to hear how Evelyn rationalized Michel telling her off.

Evelyn waved her hand like she was washing away any memory of Michel's words. "He's a passionate man. It's what I love about him. You never know what he'll say or do one minute to the next."

Brett raised his eyebrows and then slowly lowered them. There was no point in contradicting her. Evelyn didn't want to and wouldn't change. It was better for her to be wrong about Michel than to have Brett reveal the truths, truths Michel had trusted only him with. Truths he made clear he would only share with his inner circle. Evelyn, no matter how many t-shirts she made or phone cases she bedazzled, would never be in that inner circle.

"Bye, Evie," he said in response to her announcement she was going to go check out.

She rolled her eyes as a farewell and left with her suitcases, all of which were branded with Michel's photo.

Brett's heart throbbed as he watched Michel's face roll away from him. It was stupid, but he missed his face. The man was right upstairs. It hadn't been an hour since they'd quarreled and already Brett couldn't stand it. Had enough time passed?

He didn't realize Patience stayed behind until she set an elbow on the small table and fixed him with her own intense stare. "Don't worry, I won't tell her you already lost him."

Brett jumped and returned Patience's keen gaze with a scowl. "How'd you know?" he asked sullenly.

"I'm a master observer of human behavior. Never forget that," she said, not joking even one tiny bit. She turned and started to walk away. Then she stopped, turned back around to him, and said, "Oh, and Brett? Watch your back. Someone on this island has it in for you."

She was gone before Brett could ask her what the hell she was talking about. He considered running after her to find out more but knew it could be playing right into her game.

A minute later, it didn't matter. A minute later, the person she was talking about walked into the bar.

If Brett were to make a list of the top ten people who might hold a grudge against him, Lauren Fontile, or whatever her name was these days, would be at the top. Followed by Simon Anton on a bad day, then Simon Anton on a good day. But no matter how much Simon enjoyed making snide comments about him, he was nowhere near Lauren Fontile.

The last time Brett had seen her had been at the film premiere when he'd reunited with Michel and met Lucille. The other events of the evening had eclipsed his meeting with Lauren until this moment. Now, as she made a beeline for him, a knockout in a strapless red dress and silvery blond hair, he remembered.

"Well, well, well. Brett Jacobs," she purred as she reached him, her gentle tone hiding thinly veiled daggers.

"Lauren," Brett said, his voice weak. He tried to pull himself together, to act like one of the Antons—cool and dangerous, unruffled by the appearance of his former agent whose career he'd destroyed. "I haven't seen you since the premiere."

Lauren laughed, showing her brilliant white smile, a smile that failed to reach her stony gray eyes. "No, but I've seen you."

"Because"—Brett gulped— "you've been spying on me?"

Lauren laughed again, the sound delicate and well-crafted, a piece of artisan mirth. "I hardly call it spying to coincidentally vacation at the same resort. After all, I've had this trip planned for months. How was I to know you'd be here at the same time?"

Brett relaxed a little. "So, you didn't come here because you want to get back at me."

"No, Brett. My visit has nothing to do with you. What a ridiculous suggestion. Do you think I've spent all this time waiting to what, get revenge on you? Who does that?"

Brett sighed. "I'm sorry. It's been a hard day."

He didn't trust her. He wasn't going to make that mistake again. But it did seem ludicrous to assume she'd been seeking vengeance. Ludicrous and completely self-centered. More of his paranoia. The same paranoia and anxiety that drove Michel away and destined him to be alone on this bar stool, utterly destitute and miserable.

"No offense taken. Now, why don't you and I have a drink and catch up? Put all of that behind us and get to know each other again?" Lauren leaned into him when she spoke, her eyes softening, her smile back.

Brett leaned away and fixed his gaze firmly on his empty glass. "Um, I'm not great company right now."

"I don't mind. I'm a good listener."

He shouldn't give in. He shouldn't agree. But what else was he doing? Michel didn't want to be around him. He couldn't leave the island, since they'd arrived in Michel's plane. It wasn't like he had to tell Lauren anything. He could have a drink and listen to her talk about her fabulous new life and call it a day. Maybe by that time, Michel would let him back into the room, to get his suitcase if nothing else. What a dark thought.

So, he nodded. "Yes, all right."

He waved to a server. "Another for me and—" He turned to Lauren.

"Banana rum with a splash of pineapple juice, on ice."

Brett held back his disgust. It had to be the grossest drink order he'd ever heard, and he'd had some pretty gross stuff during his drinking days.

The server, no doubt used to tourists ordering anything and everything remotely tropical, just nodded and served the drinks.

"Do you want to sit?" Brett asked, gesturing to the empty stool across from him.

"Let's go somewhere a little more private," Lauren suggested.

Brett agreed, not sure what she meant but guessing it was away from the listening ears of the staff. He couldn't argue there, especially if anything from their past came up during the conversation. He followed her across the restaurant and through a door on the far side of the terrace.

"I thought this was a private event room or something," Brett said.

"It is."

That seemed to be all the explanation Lauren was going to give him.

The door led to a smaller copy of the restaurant. A few high-top tables scattered around a smooth, dark, tiled floor. A smaller aquarium bar sat against the wall, equally well-stocked but missing bartenders. Along the opposite wall were full-length windows overlooking the pool and beyond, the ocean. Either the day had turned cloudy outside or the windows were tinted. Brett frowned at them.

"No one can see in from outside," Lauren said, settling onto a stool at one of the high tops.

"That's strange," Brett said, sitting down opposite her and setting his soda water on the highly polished wood table.

"I'd imagine if you were having a private event, you wouldn't want everyone at the pool staring at you." Lauren crossed one leg over the other, a feat Brett would have guessed was impossible in her tight dress but one she handled with ease.

Brett nodded.

"So, tell me everything you've been up to, Brett. I hear you're a scientist?"

Brett looked at her, at her ageless face, her shiny, frizz-free hair, and her unreadable gray eyes framed by smoky eyeshadow. There was something off, but he couldn't put his finger on what it was. Her interest in him, her cheerful, casual attitude, both were certainly odd, but that wasn't it. Maybe it was the fact she was talking to him at all?

"Are you sure you aren't upset about what happened with Lou and the contract and the whole blacklisting thing?" he asked before thinking it through. It was a dangerous question but Brett needed the answer before the conversation continued any further. If she was upset, he shouldn't be sitting with her in a private room where no one knew he was. Perhaps, though, it was what he deserved.

He deserved to feel the force of her anger, to sit and hear her out if that was what she wanted. And it wasn't like it could make him feel any worse than he already did.

"Not at all. I was upset, but it's in the past." She raised her glass. "To new beginnings."

Brett followed suit. "New beginnings," he said and took a drink of his soda water. It didn't taste right. "I think the bartender put alcohol in..."

He trailed off as the poison Lauren had slipped into his glass took effect.

Chapter Twenty-Two

Brett had never drunk poison before, so he didn't know whether the effects were normal or not. He also didn't know what kind of poison it was nor what size of a dose Lauren had given him. These were questions a medical professional would want answers to, should one happen to materialize in time to save him. Brett should do some research. Just in case. He might be dying, but he was still a scientist, dammit.

His thoughts cut off abruptly as his body convulsed.

His lungs constricted even as he tried to force air into them. He gasped, desperate to keep breathing as his throat closed. Whether these were the symptoms of death by poisoning or symptoms of his panic about his death by poisoning, he didn't know.

Another spasm racked through him.

He blinked at the fuzzy image of Lauren Fontile sitting across the table and smiling in what he thought was a cruel way. "What did you give me?" he choked, and his voice sounded distant, like it belonged to someone else and that person was underwater.

Lauren laughed, the harshness of her laugh cutting through the fog and stinging Brett's ears. "I suppose there's no harm in telling you now. You'll be dead before anyone can get to you."

Brett frowned, or thought he did. Weren't villains supposed to monologue before they delivered the fatal blow? Weren't they supposed to talk for so long the hero's friends had time to arrive and conquer the foe? Lauren hadn't waited. She'd gotten him alone and vulnerable, slipped the poison in his glass, and waited for him to drink it.

It was all wrong. Not at all according to plan. The plan where Brett found out who'd been messing with his life, made up with Michel, and lived happily ever after. The plan where Brett didn't die.

"It's cyanide," the shape of Lauren said.

Was it just him or did she say *cyanide*? The word echoed in his ears, reverberating off the walls of his brain as it struggled for oxygen. There was no mistaking the echo, it was clearly saying *cyanide*.

If Brett were in a better head space, he'd have a hundred jokes about this. Who used cyanide poisoning outside of an old-timey detective novel? Or a spy movie where the agents were all told to take cyanide capsules if they were caught and questioned. Where did someone even *get* cyanide these days? Someone who wasn't a chemist or meth maker. Brett didn't know for sure if people who made meth had cyanide handy, but it seemed more logical for them to have it than his former agent. Then again, she was married to some lord or something now, so maybe she thought she'd gone back in time?

This is good stuff, Brett's brain managed to tell him. He should write it down and maybe he'd have enough content to write that sequel film. That would show Lauren. He'd write the sequel and she wouldn't get a penny of the proceeds.

Somehow, during this jumbled rambling of his thoughts, Brett found himself on the floor. He couldn't remember getting off the chair or falling. He couldn't be certain it was the floor, but it was hard and pressed against the length of his back. It felt cool and smooth.

Voices. Lauren had been talking, and maybe she realized she'd done things backward. If this was her monologue and she wanted him to hear it, it was too late. He wasn't listening.

Someone said his name, and he didn't think it was Lauren. The voice was too emotional, too familiar. He tried to force his eyes open, but his brain wasn't sending messages well and he could only manage a squint. Blurry light, shapes, vague recognition of Michel, and someone else. Noah? They were there and they were the people he needed to tell about the cyanide, the people who could save him.

He convulsed into a black nothingness.

Lucille burst through the door of the private event room, followed by Noah and Michel in his bathrobe. She'd expected the situation to be bad, but not this bad. The tall, vaguely familiar woman in the red dress, standing, no, gloating, over a convulsing, dying Brett. The woman, Lauren, turned, saw them, and ran for the patio door. She was fast, but Lucille's reaction time was faster. She'd taken in the scene, guessed Lauren would run, and reached the door first. Lauren looked at her in surprise and Lucille used those brief moments of shock to corner her.

Across the room, Michel grabbed Noah's arm and they ran to where Brett lay, spasming on the floor. As they approached, Michel dropped Noah's arm and fell into a beautifully graceful slide, coming to a stop right next to his dying lover. Noah performed more of an awkward falling-to-his-knees action and ended up banging his right knee against the floor and grimacing at the pain. He kneeled on the opposite side of Brett from Michel, staring down at the man who was showing signs of—

"Cyanide poisoning," Michel said in a brusque voice.

Noah blinked. "How do you know that?"

"He's exhibiting all the classic symptoms," Michel said and started to list them.

"But...how do you know that?"

Michel gave him an intense look Noah interpreted to mean, "I'll tell you when my boyfriend isn't dying." Then he said, in perfect, unironic seriousness, "I have the antidote on me."

Noah had been preparing to do CPR. He didn't quite remember how to do it but knew he needed to get Brett breathing again. Luckily, his questionable CPR skills weren't needed as the next second, Michel whipped open his bathrobe and pulled out a gold, old-fashioned cigarette case from the inside pocket. Inside the case were a number of loaded syringes, each with tiny labels on them. He grabbed one, deftly rolled up Brett's sleeve, and stabbed the needle in his arm, pressing until the syringe was empty. Brett stilled.

There was no way this was really happening. Noah gaped at Michel. "Why the fuck do you carry around a bunch of syringes?"

Michel watched Brett, grasping the dying man's arm. "I grabbed them when we left the room."

"But...why do you have them in the first place?"

"It's something I do," said Michel, his voice strained and clipped. "Now could you save the questions for later? I need to see if it worked."

Noah dutifully closed his mouth, pushing back the rest of his curiosity. He knew Michel was eccentric but carrying around poison antidotes seemed a bit more than that. Still, if his eccentricity saved Brett's life, what did it matter why?

He made a mental note to ask Michel how often people tried to poison him and what they could do to stop it.

A few tense seconds passed, punctuated by the loud, violent confrontation taking place across the floor, a confrontation that seemed to have no sense of the gravity they were dealing with.

Brett suddenly inhaled, his whole chest rising with the force of his breath. Noah thought it might be the longest breath he'd ever witnessed. Finally,

Brett exhaled and then began to breathe normally. But he didn't wake up. Noah glanced at Michel and saw, for what he now realized was the first time ever, real fear in the celebrity's eyes.

Leaving Noah and Michel to take care of Brett and hoping they wouldn't fuck it up, Lucille faced her trapped foe.

"Lauren Cunningham." Lucille fell into her role with ease. She was tempted to tell Lauren to pick on someone her own size instead of preying on Brett but knew it wouldn't deliver the punch she was looking for. "Really? You? I would have thought it was someone with a little more at stake."

Lauren, her back to the tinted windows, stopped looking around the room, for an escape no doubt, and fixed her glare on Lucille. Then she charged, hitting Lucille squarely in the gut. Lucille grunted but stayed her ground. She slid her hands between her body and the kicking, scratching agent, and pushed as hard as she could. Lauren stumbled back and hit the floor.

A moment later, she regained her footing, took a deep breath, and smoothed her dress. Lucille planted her feet in preparation for another attack, but it seemed Lauren was changing tactics.

"Who the hell are you?" Lauren asked, her voice biting and cold. She looked Lucille up and down, clearly trying to make her feel self-conscious and insecure.

But this woman didn't know who she was dealing with. Lucille's life was filled with celebrity clients trying to make her insignificant to boost their own perceived superiority. She'd been raised by a mother who specialized in that kind of treatment. Yes, there were a few people who could get inside her poised exterior—Simon, sometimes Brett, Michel, and, damn him, Noah. But not this woman, not Lauren Cunningham. Lucille waited until Lauren had given up her attempt at an eviscerating stare before she responded. "Aw, that's cute. You've never heard of me. I thought you knew everyone in the business, Lauren. I can call you Lauren, right? Great. It's so much easier than remembering all of your last names."

Lauren's eyes flashed with anger so quickly, Lucille wouldn't have noticed it if they weren't engaged in an intense stare-down. Then it was gone, and Lauren's face was a cold, hard shell, a mirror of Lucille's. She stalked forward, closing the distance between them.

Lucille didn't move. She wasn't intimidated by Lauren and wouldn't be. She knew what this was.

She was, however, petrified about what was happening to Brett. The background snippets of conversation she could hear from Noah and Michel weren't exactly comforting.

"I know everyone of importance in Hollywood," Lauren said, still advancing until she was right in Lucille's face, her stilettos putting her a good inch higher than Lucille's strappy platforms. "And since I don't know you, it means you must be a no one."

Lucille smiled, slowly and dangerously. "When's the last time you had clients, Lauren?"

Lauren laughed, a cold laugh. "Clients. How silly. I don't need clients. I have a whole new business now."

"Oh?" Lucille wanted to feign interest but found herself actually intrigued. "And what's that? Poisoning people?"

Lauren laughed again. "Gold-digging."

Lucille couldn't help herself, she was impressed. "Really."

"Oh, yes. It's an excellent business. I marry rich men, take their money, and move on," Lauren said candidly, "It was a shame when Lord Cunningham died while we were married, but I must say, it was nice to not have to go through the divorce proceedings for once."

Lucille almost lost her composure but pulled herself together before any of it showed on her face. It was the meeting with Sylvia all over again. She'd gone in expecting to find a heartless bitch and had left with a new friend. One who could match her for being cold, calculating, and always on top. "I have to say, that's brilliant."

"I know." Lauren's smile became a little more genuine.

"Maybe if things were different, we could have been friends. I am always looking for ways to expand my business," Lucille said, feeling a warmth toward Lauren she couldn't quite repress.

"What's your business?" Lauren asked, matching the warmth, her gray eyes gentler.

"Lucille Anton, Celebrity Spin Doctor."

"No," Lauren gasped. "Really? I-I mean of course I've heard of you, but I never knew what you looked like. No one did."

Lucille smiled smugly. She wanted to preen a little, then get down to the details of how she might be able to incorporate gold digging as a branch of the celebrity spin doctor empire.

But it was not to be.

"Lucille. What the fuck are you doing?" Noah hissed from somewhere to her right.

Right. Brett. Brett is dying. She was back. She shook her head sadly. "But you had to go after Brett, didn't you? Couldn't let that one go, could you?"

Lauren's friendliness drained away. "Why do you care? He's not one of your clients, is he?"

"God no. He's one of my best friends," Lucille said, "and the only ex-boyfriend I'm still on speaking terms with. I'm pretty invested in him living."

"That's unfortunate. Because he's going to die."

"No, he's not," Michel said, "I had an antidote."

"What?" Lauren said, and this time, her voice came out as a screech. She evidently hadn't counted on anyone, if they did come to help Brett, having an antidote.

Lucille herself was surprised. Michel was unpredictable, but to carry around poison antidotes? Actually, no, it made a lot of sense for Michel. After all, only a few months ago, Sylvia had threatened his life regularly and those precautionary habits were, Lucille could imagine, hard to break.

Lucille shook her head. "Vengeance never works, Lauren. Should've stuck with what you were good at."

Lauren launched herself at Lucille again, this time with an enraged growl. Lucille had good instincts but not good enough to block an opponent at close range. Lauren hit her hard and they both fell backward onto the smooth, tiled floor. Lauren was wild with fury, her hands a flurry of clawing and tugging.

Lucille put her arms up to protect her face. She was on the bottom and hadn't been able to cushion herself on impact. Her left hip and elbows had taken most of the damage, luckily not her head. *This is why I'm never on bottom*, she thought as her surprise turned to annoyance. With a grunt of pain, she lifted her right knee up and used it to push Lauren off.

It worked in part, then someone else, Noah, she guessed, stepped forward and grabbed Lauren's flailing arms.

Lucille didn't waste time lying on the floor. It may be a private room, but it was still a restaurant. She got to her feet as gracefully as she could, her elbows stinging, her back protesting, and her knee smarting. Her abs ached from the first hit. Still, the pain didn't even begin to compare to being shot, so she ignored her bruises, tossed her hair, and surveyed the fallout.

It wasn't Noah who restrained Lauren Cunningham. It was a man in a security uniform, trying to get her under control while a man in a suit talked to her. The resort manager, if Lucille had to guess. She gave them a zero out of ten on their response. After all, as soon as they'd landed, she'd called the main office and told them to contact whatever local police they had immediately. And they were only now arriving. Men.

She turned and caught Noah's eye. He raised his eyebrows at her, as if to ask if she was okay. Like he cared. As if she cared if he did or not. She nodded so he'd stop looking at her.

For reasons completely unknown, he left the room.

Beyond Noah lay Brett, still on the floor but not jerking around anymore. Michel kneeled over him, rubbing his cheek. The gesture was so tender, the moment so achingly sweet, Lucille had to look away.

She approached the man in the suit. As she drew closer, she saw he was, in fact, the resort manager. Charles, according to his name tag. He broke off at her approach, turning to stare at her with wide eyes.

"What took so long?" Lucille demanded, not in the mood to play games.

"I-I apologize, ma'am. We've never had an incident like this and, well, there are rules to follow and protocols—"

He hadn't believed her. Hadn't believed her when she said there was a dangerous guest at his resort, one who was intent on harming another guest. There was no way everything was perfect all the time at The Reef, not with the type of clientele they catered to. But Lucille wasn't going to care what this man thought and wasn't about to listen to him stammer out an explanation.

"We don't have time for any of that. This woman is wanted by the feds—"

"What? No, I'm not," Lauren protested.

"After JP Tanaka called and told them about you? Yes, you are," Lucille said, perfunctorily. She hadn't mentioned it earlier, wanting to keep Lauren talking. Now Lauren was the hotel's problem. They could keep her in check until the government officials arrived.

The color drained from Lauren's face.

It was a shame. Maybe she'd reach out to Lauren later, help her get back on her feet after she got through whatever punishment she was dealt for attempted murder.

For now, though. "This man"—she gestured to Brett— "needs medical attention immediately. He's been poisoned."

"Oh, my God, I didn't realize," the hotel manager exclaimed, trying to move in multiple directions at once. "I thought this doctor was caring for him."

Lucille was exhausted. "That's Michel Polce. Not a doctor."

At the sound of his name, Michel looked up.

The manager's eyes grew, if possible, even wider. He finally pulled his shit together and soon the room bustled with activity. A protesting Lauren was led away by the security guard. An actual doctor arrived and pushed Michel aside to examine the unconscious Brett. The manager glommed onto Lucille, asking her endless questions about what happened and whether she was going to sue.

Lucille took a seat at the high-top table where the two glasses still stood, as though waiting for the intermission to be over and the scene to resume. She ignored the manager's questions so completely she didn't notice he'd stopped talking to her until another voice replaced his chatter.

"Lucille."

She glanced up to find Noah in front of her, his expression one of guarded concern.

"You're bleeding," he said and handed her a martini.

Chapter Twenty-Three

Brett opened his eyes. He didn't want to open them. The lids were heavy and took more effort to lift than he remembered eyelids requiring. He could tell, even partway through the movement, the light was too bright and would hurt. But he'd sensed someone watching him for a while now, since he'd regained consciousness in fact, and he needed to see what all that was about. So, he forced them open and found Lucille staring at him.

"Oh, good, you're not dead," she said.

"No," Brett said, forcing the words out of his throat with a great deal of effort. Had talking always been so hard? He didn't think it had. "But I feel like death."

"On a scale of you on a normal day to being pushed down the stairs at Michel's, how does this death feeling rate?"

Brett closed his eyes again. They were too heavy. He hoped, if Lucille was going to stick around and talk to him for a while longer, she'd be okay with him not looking at her. "Worse than falling down the stairs."

"That is bad."

"Why did you think I was dead?"

"Do you not remember being poisoned?"

As she said it, Brett did remember. The glass on the high-top table. Lauren's friendly olive branch turning out to be a ruse, one he'd fallen for so, so easily. He remembered the pain of dying and then nothing. "Oh. That. Yeah, I remember. So, I didn't die?"

"Not quite. You were close, but Michel had an antidote."

If Brett could have made his head nod, he would've nodded. "That makes sense."

If there were anyone who would carry around an antidote for a poison no one had used in years, it'd be Michel. Well, Michel or a doctor who specialized in poison control. All these rambling thoughts were beside the point. The point was Michel had the antidote and Brett hadn't died. Which was cool. "Michel was there?"

He forced his eyelids back open and even turned his head, another feat that took enormous effort, to look at Lucille.

She sat in a chair beside the bed he was lying in, since, with his eyes open, he could tell he was lying down and when he turned his head, he could see part of a pillow and some blankets. Lucille, her face calm but her gaze holding worry Brett had never seen before, was drinking a martini. "Of course Michel was there. Why didn't you tell him we were coming to the island? And why did you go into a private room with Lauren Cunningham? Didn't you know she was trying to kill you?"

"Are you yelling at me? I just died." Brett winced, wishing Lucille wouldn't talk so loudly. Her questions didn't make sense. He wasn't certain where he was. A room, a familiar room with some extremely brightly painted walls. He was in a room with a bed and Lucille was yelling at him.

"*Almost* died. You almost died."

Brett ignored the correction. "What are you even talking about? You didn't tell me you were coming and Lauren was perfectly civil to me."

"Right up until she slipped you some poison?"

"Well, yes," Brett admitted. "At that point, things changed a little. Where is she, anyway?"

"Arrested. And she won't be getting off on a technicality and going to a secret rehab or anything. She made the mistake of crossing me and JP," Lucille said as though that explained things.

"Oh," Brett said like he understood. As long as Lauren wasn't going to try killing him again, he'd worry about the details later. He tried to piece together the rest of the events. "Who else was there? I think I remember another person."

"Noah," said Lucille and her voice was suddenly harsh and clipped.

"Really?" Brett made an attempt at widening his eyes in surprise but it hurt his aching head and he stopped. "Does that mean…"

"It means nothing."

He didn't believe her for a second. "I knew it. From the moment you two met at the not-sex party, there was something. Totally called that one."

He expected Lucille to protest and/or smother him with his pillow. When she did neither, merely stared into her martini, he knew she had it bad. Lucille Anton wasn't one to pass up the chance to retort.

"We didn't meet at the party." Her voice was a touch too loud, also very out of character.

"You didn't? But how did you…where would you…" His brain refused to complete his thoughts. He trailed off and waited.

Lucille still hadn't looked up from her glass. "Do you remember the lemur rescue event I did when we were in San Francisco?"

Brett did and said so.

"Well, I met Noah there."

"Ah. So that's how he knew who you were."

"Yes. And I didn't just meet him. I made out with him."

"Sure. You made out with a hot guy at a party, as you do." It all made a lot of sense to Brett and he'd suffered a near-death experience earlier that same day. Noah must not be nearly as smart as he looked.

"He accused me of cheating on you and being a heartless bitch."

Noah really wasn't as smart as he looked. "Whoa."

"I know."

"Heartless bitch, yes. But we were broken up."

"Which I told him."

Brett thought about it for a bit. In the silence, he could hear the ocean outside the open windows. He did his best to connect the timeline. First their move to San Francisco, then their first break-up a few weeks later, then a few more break-ups after that... the charity event would have happened sometime between those break-ups and when they went to help Simon find Michel. It checked out. And confirmed Noah was an idiot if he lost Lucille over something as inane as timing.

He forced himself to look at Lucille, to get his neck back in the habit of moving again. She was staring down at her now empty glass, looking surprisingly maudlin. It wasn't an expression Brett thought the Antons could make, which explained why he was slow to make the connection. "Wait a second. You care, don't you? You really care about what Noah thinks of you."

The maudlin Lucille was gone in an instant, replaced by the glaring Lucille he was used to. "I do *not* care about what Noah Harkin thinks about a damn thing."

Brett laughed, even though it hurt his head and lungs. "Yes, you do. You like him. Like really like him."

Lucille glared more but didn't deny it. "This isn't about me and it certainly has nothing to do with Noah. The real question is what the hell happened between you and Michel. Full story. Now."

Brett's chest hurt. "I think I'm having a heart attack."

"No, you're not. You're avoiding."

"You know, you're the worst person to have around in a medical crisis."

"Excuse me. I got a doctor to make sure you were going to live, didn't I?"

Brett gestured to the room with a heavy hand. "Yes, but did you take me to a hospital?"

"You didn't need a hospital. The doctor said you'd be fine."

Brett made a note to himself not to be around any Antons the next time he was gravely injured. He might not survive their brand of medical care again. "Speaking of Michel, where is he? Did he go out to get coffee or something?"

Lucille frowned and didn't respond.

"Lucille," Brett said in what he wanted to be a serious tone but which still sounded weak. "Where's Michel?"

"You don't remember talking to him? About two hours ago?"

"What?"

"Actually, talking doesn't cover it. You don't remember shouting at him two hours ago?" Lucille looked at him like he'd lost his mind and, after hearing this tidbit of information, she might not be wrong.

"I did what?" He tried to shout and ended up coughing, his throat burning.

"I don't know the whole story but from what I heard through the wall and the brief recap Michel gave me afterward, you woke up, or appeared to wake up. Michel was by the bed and when you saw him, you lost it. You were yelling that now you needed space and he'd better respect your goddamn boundaries because, and I quote, 'if you can't get space when you die, when can you?'"

"What's that supposed to mean?"

Lucille shook her head. "I have no fucking clue. You upset Michel pretty badly though."

If Brett thought he felt poorly before, it was nothing compared to his current state. His heart throbbed, his vision starting to blur, his whole body seemed too big, too exposed, and yet he couldn't shrink it. He blinked until the motion made him dizzy. "I don't remember any of that."

"Yeah, I got that."

He didn't want to ask, but dammit, he needed to know. He looked at her with his most pleading expression, begging her to answer honestly. "So...where is he?"

"Oh, he took his plane back to his house. He said you didn't seem to be very coherent and that you were probably having some warped flashbacks of your earlier argument. He said to come around when you get back and are thinking more clearly," said Lucille lightly.

The panic washed out of Brett as quickly as it had arrived. "Lucille," he tried to yell and coughed instead.

When he got the coughing under control, he continued the yelling. "Why the fuck didn't you start with that?"

"I had to see if you'd meant what you said or if it really was some sort of near-death paranoia. I don't want either of you getting hurt."

Perhaps he still wasn't coherent because Lucille's explanation made a lot of sense. It was actually a sweet gesture. For her. And now he was getting choked up on top of everything else. "You're my best friend, you know that, right?"

"I thought Michel was your best friend."

"You're my best friend who isn't Michel."

Lucille laughed. Brett tried to join in but stopped when his muscles protested fiercely. Instead, he lay on the hotel room bed in the tropical suite and grinned.

After a minute of companionable silence, Lucille stood and set her empty glass on the nightstand. "As fun as this is, let's get off this damn island. Do you think you can travel?"

Brett moved his limbs experimentally. "I better be able to. I've got to go run after Michel. Figuratively, obviously."

"Obviously. Noah's supposed to be getting the plane ready."

"I thought Michel took the plane."

"How do you think we got here, Brett? By boat?"

"Okay, now you're just being mean to a guy who's recently survived a poisoning and possibly a mild heart attack."

Lucille shook her head and turned to leave.

"Lucille?" Brett called.

She turned back.

"Thank you."

"Anytime." She rolled her eyes, smiled, and headed for the door.

"Oh, and, Luce?"

This time, she didn't smile when she turned. "What now?"

"Don't be so hard on Noah. He likes you, too," Brett said, exuding wisdom and generosity.

"Brett."

"Yes?" Here it came. The heartfelt thank-you for helping her uncover her real feelings about Noah.

"Shut up."

CHAPTER TWENTY-FOUR

*D*ammit, *Brett,* Lucille thought as she took the elevator down to the lobby. Since he was going to make a full recovery, presumably, she felt no remorse for cursing him and his stupid insight into her life. Although, to be honest, which she wasn't, she'd been thinking about giving Noah a real chance ever since he brought her the martini. He hadn't tried to talk over her or coddle her in any way. He'd gotten her the one thing she actually needed at the moment without asking. She wasn't foolish enough to let him walk away because he said dumb shit when he was hurt and upset, was she?

Sure, she didn't say dumb shit when she was hurt and upset, but she did freeze people out, and was her coping method superior to his?

Yes, it was decidedly superior. It didn't mean she couldn't forgive him.

Noah waited for her in the lobby, sitting on a tropical-print bench across from the front desk, looking at something on his phone. Like the hypervigilant former PI he was, he noticed her immediately and came to meet her.

"How's Brett?" he asked, frowning. Noah had managed to come out of the confrontation largely unscathed, which was more than Lucille could say for herself. She desperately needed a change of clothes and a strong antibacterial for her fingernail-induced wounds.

She raised her eyebrow at him. After all, it'd been only that morning he'd yelled at her about coming to save Brett. Now he was worried about the guy's wellbeing?

"What?"

She shook her head. "He'll live. I have no idea if he's okay to travel, but I don't think any of us want to hang out at this place much longer. How's the plane?"

Noah nodded. "Good. The resort manager is also very eager for us to go and had our plane readied even before I asked."

"Fine. I'll get someone to retrieve Brett and meet you at the airstrip in a few minutes." Lucille took a step toward the desk when Noah's hand on her arm stopped her. She looked down at his hand, his round nails, long, brown, skillful fingers...

"Are you okay?" he said softly, too low for anyone to overhear.

The gentleness in his voice nearly crumbled her martini-fueled strength. For a second, and only a second, she considered sinking into his arms. Letting out all the stress and strain of the day and letting him hold her. The strength of the urge unnerved her.

She blinked hard and pulled her arm away. "Of course," she said, not looking making eye contact.

This was not the time nor place. The deep conversations and second chances, if they got to those, were going to have to wait.

They landed in LA in the evening. It wasn't until she'd found an airport employee to help wrangle Brett from the plane to the hired car that she realized Noah wasn't getting off. He was, apparently, returning with the plane to San Francisco.

She didn't know why she was surprised. He lived in San Francisco. Yes, he'd left some clothing at her house, but it was nothing he couldn't come back for later. He'd visited the city to meet with Sylvia, that was all. And as much as he worked with both of them, he was Simon's protégé, so it would be only right he'd go back to Simon when all was said and done.

They hadn't made any promises to each other. They hadn't even made plans. They weren't a couple. There was no Lucille and Noah.

So why did it hurt when he didn't say goodbye?

Then again, Lucille didn't say goodbye either. She didn't do goodbyes.

Brett, for his part, was entirely concerned with when his head would stop pounding so he could embark on his ridiculously romantic reunion with Michel. With all the confusing emotions of a movie montage overlaid with a Sarah McLaughlin song, Lucille and Brett drove to her house.

She intended to make a plan of all the things she needed to do for her clients, all the ways she could up her game even more. Instead, she found herself thinking of all the things she should have said to Noah. Everything she wanted him to say to her. And, mostly, why she couldn't get his stupid, cute face out of her head.

It took her a minute to realize Brett was watching her. "What?" she said with a bit more of a bite than she intended.

"That was some lame-ass goodbye at the airport. Did you make plans to see each other or talk or anything?"

Lucille narrowed her eyes and scowled at him. "No, we did not," she said with enough force to shut down any further questions on the matter.

They reached Lucille's apartment, and Brett, after declaring himself well enough to drive to Michel's, passed out on the couch.

It had been a long day, longer than a single day had any right to be, but, after napping on the plane, Lucille couldn't sleep. When the sun called in the start of a new day, she'd barely dropped off, and, when the doorbell rang, she was exhausted, crabby, and not at all interested in whatever her visitor had to say. She lay in bed, hoping they'd go away. But the bell rang again.

A more alert Lucille would have been comparing the list of people who knew where she lived to the list of people who rang doorbells. Fully alert Lucille would have created a plan of attack.

This Lucille put on a quick game face, ran a brush through her hair, threw on a robe, and prepared to kick the uninvited guest's ass.

She threw the door open, glaring at the interloper who'd woken her up.

On her doorstep stood Noah, looking like he'd slept in his clothes. He froze when he saw her, and swallowed, taking in the full appearance of her in all her early-morning glory. She had, of course, forgotten to close the robe, and her silk shorts and tank top pajama ensemble was on full display.

Her heart leaped and she almost lost her glare. But she was a professional, goddammit, and she kept it firmly in place. No matter that she'd caught feelings for this man, she wasn't about to put up with him waking her up at the ass-crack of dawn. "What the fucking hell, Noah?"

"Lucille." His voice croaked.

She waited for him to continue, but he didn't. "Well?"

"Can I come in?" he asked.

Lucille stepped aside enough to let him pass her into the house. And not just Noah but, given the number of suitcases he had with him, half his worldly belongings. "Seriously, what the hell? Yesterday you leave without a goodbye, and today you show up with all your shit?"

She wasn't being cool and collected at all.

He dragged the last of the cases inside and closed the door. Then he turned to Lucille. His body language was cagey, and he didn't meet her glare. "Lucille."

"What?"

"I need to tell you some things."

"So, tell me."

Noah fiddled with a suitcase tag. "I was wrong. I was so wrong about Brett and Michel. You were right, they did need you to save them. Although, in my defense, who the hell poisons someone because they lost them a job? That isn't normal behavior."

"Yeah, well, that kind of thing happens more often than not in this business."

"I've noticed."

She frowned. Whether it was too early in the morning or Noah wasn't being clear or, as she suspected, a mix of both, none of what he said explained the suitcases. "Okay."

"That was part one. The second part is, well, I love all of this. The back-biting celebrities, the ostentatious parties, the truly wild shit you deal with on a daily basis. And I really liked working with you these past few days. So...I'm moving here."

Lucille's heart beat faster but her brain wasn't having it. "You're moving here. As in *here* here? You're moving in with me?"

"No," he said quickly, "I mean, not right away. That seems a little...too soon. I mean, we haven't even been on a date, and there's probably a few more steps we need to get to before we think about moving in together. I'll be renting a place not far from here. Someone Simon knows."

Lucille's brain sputtered out around the date part and her heart took over completely. Well, almost completely. Aside from the moment she considered it at the hotel, she wasn't someone to fall into someone's arms. Especially when that someone hadn't told her how he felt about her and had woken her up at dawn. "What are you talking about, Noah?"

At this, Noah met her gaze. "I'm talking about us."

"Is there an us?" She was asking honestly, but it came out sounding harsh and he flinched.

"I mean, there doesn't have to be, if you don't..." he trailed off.

Dammit, I'm fucking this up. Lucille sighed. "Do you realize that you're very frustrating at times?" There was a touch of affection to her tone.

"I'm frustrating?" he retorted, and just like that, the self-doubting, vulnerable guy was gone and replaced by the confident, cocky guy she wanted to argue with and make up with and tie to a bed and do deliciously naughty things to. "You're one to talk."

A smile tugged at her mouth. She stalked forward until she was right in front of him and his back was against the door.

Noah's breath caught, his eyes blazed, and Lucille yanked his head closer and kissed him hard. He moaned into her mouth and his hands tried to grip her hips. She grabbed him by the wrists and pressed his arms firmly to his side. He obeyed and gasped as she ground against him.

Then she pushed back and looked at him.

"Does that mean yes?" he asked, breathing heavily.

"To what?"

"I don't even remember anymore."

She nodded. "Yes, yes it does."

They were still kissing against the door a few minutes later when Brett cleared his throat behind them. "Uh, don't you two have a perfectly good room to defile each other in?"

Lucille let go of one of Noah's arms only long enough to give Brett the finger, then went back to feeling Noah up.

"Really mature, Luce. Will you at least move out of the way so I can get to the door?"

At that, Lucille did break away. She glanced over at Brett. He seemed refreshed after his ordeal—energized, impatient, and showered. He was dressed in a navy-blue suit with a crisp pink shirt underneath. Michel's favorite colors. She wondered where he'd gotten the outfit. As far as she knew, Brett did not own a navy suit.

"Are those my clothes?" Noah asked. Lucille could feel his voice vibrating through his chest.

"Yes, do you mind if I borrow them?" Brett asked, glancing down at himself.

"I guess not," Noah replied with a shrug that scraped his chest against her sensitized breasts. She clenched against the desire to squirm into him. She wished Brett would go away, but a part of her was concerned about whether Brett was doing as well as he looked.

"How are you feeling?"

Brett set his jaw. "Much better. I'm going to get my man back."

Lucille was still holding her body tense or she would have laughed at how sincere and serious Brett looked. "It's been less than a day. How can you have possibly recovered from almost dying already?"

Brett deflated. "Yes, right. I suppose I should rest here today and make extra sure I'm better. You won't mind me hanging around with you two for another day or so?"

Noah's fingers tightened on her hip.

Lucille backtracked quickly. "Nope, I was wrong. You look absolutely the picture of health. Go get him."

Brett brightened. "Okay, but if I collapse on the way there..."

Noah's voice was desperate when he spoke. "Then we'll come find you. Get going, Brett, no time to lose."

Brett nodded once and walked out the door, his shoulders squared and his hands trembling.

When the door closed, Lucille grabbed Noah by the lapels of his jacket and pulled him until their faces were a centimeter apart. "Thank God. Noah, I swear, if we don't have sex right now, I'm going to explode."

Noah matched her in intensity, heat, and roving hands. "Lead the way, Ms. Anton."

Chapter Twenty-Five

When the car stopped outside Michel's mansion, Brett thought he might pass out, and not just from the poisoning the day before. He knew Lucille and Noah had only told him to leave because they wanted to have sex all day, and he wondered if he really was well enough to be out and about. If he wasn't, though, being cared for and fussed over by Michel sounded far more pleasant than hanging around the couple in the first passionate throes of their coupledom.

A horrible thought followed this daydream. What if Lucille was wrong and Michel had believed his incoherent ramblings? What if Michel was broken-hearted and didn't want to see him ever again?

His anxiety returned in a ferocious tidal wave.

Michel's mansion. He hadn't been there often, but each time he'd visited had been memorable. He'd been there when Michel was ambushed daily by

Sylvia. He'd almost been murdered in the house, a couple of times. It was the house where shit had gone down, where Simon and Lucille had saved their asses from Sylvia, from Danielle, and from themselves. Yet he'd never been as nervous about going inside as he was at that moment. Not when he was kidnapped by his cousin and led into the house blindfolded. Not when he'd opened the door and found the police standing on the doorstep. None of that mattered compared to what he was about to do. He was fairly sure Michel knew he loved him, that he loved Brett in return. But to show up un-invited, nervous, and uncertain, to put his heart on the line when the last time they'd seen each other he'd deliriously told Michel to leave him alone? It was terrifying.

Brett forced himself to get out of the car. He stood on the gravel drive, took a deep breath, and straight-ened his jacket. Noah was bigger than him, a little taller, more muscular, and the suit wasn't a perfect fit. Then again, none of his own suits fit him well, so the distinction was negligible.

It took all his confidence to walk to the front door and ring the bell.

From inside, he heard a muffled thump.

No answer.

He rang again and knocked for good measure. Still no answer.

Brett frowned. Where was Michel? Was he ignoring him? Someone was in there, but maybe they couldn't hear him?

He tried the handle and found the door open. Brett pushed it open and awkwardly stepped inside.

The interior of the pristine mansion was in shambles. The railing of the marble staircase had been bashed in and pieces of wood littered the stone floor. The wall separating the main entryway from the study had also been attacked. There were huge gouges in the plaster, wires hanging out of them and support beams poking through. Debris covered everything, huge chunks of wall that had been left where they fell. From the back of the house came the distinct, rhythmic thump of a large hammer.

Brett gaped. It looked like someone had broken in and wrecked up the place. But who?

He slid down the marble hall, his shoes slippery on the stone. The hammering grew louder, as did the thundering of Brett's pulse. He'd been in this house when something bad was happening or had happened to Michel too many times not to immediately imagine all the worst-case scenarios. Sylvia deciding she wasn't over her obsession with Michel and coming back to kill him once and for all. Danielle of the crime club out of her high-end prison and trying again to lure Simon back by killing Michel. Lauren getting the ultimate revenge on him by killing Michel. Jesus, why did everyone want to kill Michel? Someday, Brett was going to have to sit down and have a chat with him about it, but right now, he desperately needed to get to the man and make sure he was alive.

Brett skidded to a halt in the living room, at the edge of the ornate rug. He was close. The hammering came from nearby. His gaze darted around the room, taking in the familiar furnishings and finally coming to rest on the swing door leading to the summer kitchen. He ran to it and threw it open.

There, wearing tight jeans and no shirt and looking like the male stripper version of a construction worker, stood Michel. He wielded a giant sledgehammer and was so intent on attacking the now crumbling wall of the summer kitchen that he didn't seem to realize he was no longer alone.

"Michel," Brett cried in between hammer strikes, ignoring how the loud pounding threatened his still-tender head.

Michel didn't drop the hammer on his foot, like Brett would have. Instead, he lowered it and turned, blinking at Brett, sweat glistening on his brow and down his abs. "Brett?"

"What are you doing?" Brett asked, unable to tear his gaze from the sight of hot, sweaty Michel.

Michel frowned like he didn't understand the question. "I could ask you the same thing."

"I came here to find you. You appear to be destroying your house."

Michel looked at the wall with the holes punched in it. "This? Just a little DIY."

"You knocked out the railing of your staircase and half a wall in the vestibule," Brett said. He stood in the doorway, gripping the handle, afraid to move closer in case Michel would back away from him. Michel was clearly upset about something, the evidence was punched into the walls.

Michel studied the hammer in his hands. "I had some things to think through."

"Things about us?" Brett's heart was in his throat now.

Michel nodded.

"And?" It was the only word he could get out. Michel didn't respond right away. Brett couldn't help himself, adding, "You should know you're very distracting in that outfit."

That got a smile and a chuckle out of his serious maybe-boyfriend. "Oh, really? Is that what you're thinking about while I'm trying to have a serious conversation about our relationship?"

Michel was smiling as he said it and Brett couldn't help but smile back.

"Michel," Brett said, loving the way his name sounded, "you're wearing the tightest jeans in the history of tight jeans and your abs are literally glistening. What am I supposed to do?"

Michel chuckled again before his smile fell away. He put down the hammer and walked through the rubble to stand in front of Brett.

Brett gasped for air but didn't move, afraid to break the spell. When Michel shoved his hands into his pockets and the movement made the fabric stretch further and bunched his muscles together, Brett forgot what breathing was.

"Michel," he whispered, "I didn't mean any of the things I said. I was delirious."

Michel nodded. "I know."

"You do? Then why are you upset and brooding?"

Brett wanted to reach out and pull Michel into his arms, to bury himself in Michel's shoulder and to share the weight of his emotions. He did the harder thing, he stood in it himself, holding it within him, ignoring the temptation to diffuse until Michel said what he needed to say.

"Because I've been thinking. People are always treating me like I'm incapable of taking care of myself. Like I don't know I have obsessed fans or like I didn't know staying with Sylvia was the wrong choice."

Brett bit his tongue against his response to the latter statement. Perhaps in retrospect, Michel could see how damaging his relationship with Sylvia had been. At the time, Brett remembered all too acutely, Michel had been all in it.

"They treat me like I need saving, like secrets need to be kept from me so I don't go off the deep end. I expect that kind of behavior from Lucille and Simon. I pay them for it. But from you? It hurt to find out you weren't only, understandably, keeping me away from your family but keeping me away from your messy past and my messy past. You almost died, Brett, and odds are it won't be the last near-death experience one of us will have. We're going to have to come up against that shit again. It's part of being who we are. But I want to be there with you, be in it with you. I want to know all your flaws and love you for them. I want to fight the bullshit in this world together, not try to keep each other safe alone."

Brett had seen every one of Michel's movies. Some of them more times than he was willing to admit. He'd cried and laughed at Michel's performances. Some of them haunted him so completely he thought he'd never be able to look at his friend again. Michel's speech, as he stood shirtless in the wreckage of his attempted DIY, was so perfect, Brett couldn't stand it. He wanted to cry and laugh and jump into Michel's arms and kiss him silly.

"I love you," he blurted out.

Michel's serious face, so sincere, so beloved, broke into a slow smile. "Does that mean you agree to my terms? You'll let me know the next time you think you might get poisoned?"

Brett blinked, then nodded solemnly. "Yes. If I suspect I'm about to be poisoned, you'll be the first person I call."

This answer seemed to satisfy Michel.

It was anyone's guess who moved first. They went from staring at each other, broken bits of wall strewn across the floor between them, then they met in the middle. Brett threw his arms around Michel, his hands running all over Michel's sweaty, muscular body, while Michel's hands worked on getting into his suit. Their mouths were hot and urgent.

Gentle kisses would come later, but for now, it was urgency and passion.

Michel walked them backward, out of the summer kitchen and into the relatively intact living room. Brett bumped into the edge of the couch and willingly collapsed onto it, pulling Michel down on top of him. Once, not that long ago, although it seemed like ancient history, Michel had reset Brett's dislocated shoulder on this couch. Now they made out like eager teenagers, groping each other in a desperate attempt to get as close as possible as fast as possible.

Then Michel broke it off, pulling back. Brett opened his eyes and frowned at the absence. He found Michel gazing down at him with heat and, there, naked on his face, love. "I love you, Brett. I don't know if you've picked up on that yet."

"I had," Brett said, his voice raspy from all the kissing. He was happy to hear the words too and showed Michel exactly how happy he was.

Afterward, as they lay gasping on the couch, Michel splayed out on top of him, Brett kissed the top of his head. "Michel? Baby?"

"Hmm?" mumbled Michel, sounding too blissed-out to respond more.

"You know we're going to have to hire someone to fix your DIY, right?"

Michel growled and the sound vibrated into Brett. "Later."

"There's a hole in your house."

Michel didn't respond for a moment. Then he sighed. "You haven't even seen what I did to the bedroom."

"I just saw you yesterday. How much could you have done?"

"I had a lot to think about, okay?"

Brett tightened his arms around Michel. He knew they'd have their ups and downs in the future. That Michel would go non-responsive when he was working on an exciting project. That Brett would work too late in the lab and miss an important occasion. They may have dealt with Lauren, but there was still his family and other people from Michel's past who would pop up at some point. Lucille would spend too much time at their house when she was annoyed with Noah, and Noah would try to get them involved in one of his espionage schemes. Plus, he had to tell JP he was moving and find a new job.

Someday, there would be weddings to plan and attend. Not that he thought Lucille and Noah would have a traditional wedding. He could see them getting married on a dare that both of them refused to back down from, ending up at a chapel in Vegas in their mutual stubbornness. Simon and JP would have an extravagant wedding, complete with sweeping vistas and custom velvet tuxes. Brett could see Simon leaving the spin doctor game and working on spy tech for JP's company. Either that or he'd continue raising hell in San Francisco, getting the rich businesspeople out of embarrassing scrapes and enjoying his life as JP's arm candy.

As for his future with Michel, Brett didn't know exactly what it would look like. Nothing as conventional as marriage and babies, not for them. Michel didn't do conventional and Brett was fully prepared to happily do whatever Michel wanted.

"I'll just sell the place and we can live off the grid in a cabin for a while," Michel said.

Within reason, that was.

"A cabin?" Brett squeaked. "But...why?"

Michel lifted his head and showed Brett his devilish grin. "I wanted to see your reaction to the suggestion."

Brett rolled his eyes.

"But I do want to move somewhere with you. This house has too many weird memories. What do you think? Somewhere we can start fresh together and argue about how many claw-foot bathtubs we should have?"

Brett leaned forward and kissed Michel gently on the lips. "I think it sounds like an excellent idea." He went in for another kiss but stopped. "Wait, how many claw-foot bathtubs are we talking here?"

Michel shook his head and pulled him in for a kiss. Brett went gladly but made a mental note to return to the bathtub subject at a later date. For now, he was content to enjoy the moment with his gorgeous, neurotic, unpredictable best friend and love.

Acknowledgements

I f it were not for Ocean's 6, this book would not have been published the first time and certainly would not be getting republished now. Alli, Brittany, Kristin, Leslie, and Scarlett, you have no idea how much your continued support means to me, how much it keeps me writing even then the going feels impossible, and how much I look forward to every one of our chats, retreats, and ad hoc brainstorm sessions.

Thank you to all of my beta readers who have helped me catch plot holes and unintentional character name changes. Thank you to Audrey for editing out my numerous errors and Najla for taking my rambling ideas and turning them into a kickass cover.

And, of course, thank you to my family. Mom and Papa for encouraging me and supporting my writing career from the beginning. Tara and Hannah for listening to my ideas, giving me last minute edits, and for all those summers we spent reading in the parents' living room. Thank you to my fur babies for the cuddles, comfort, and judgmental stares when I'm writing instead of giving them pets.

ABOUT

Celia Mulder, one of the pennames used by author C Mulder, hails from the lovely, yet unpredictable northern Michigan. They are a librarian, a former wedding planner, and an avid appreciator of all things campy and ridiculous. Friends-to-lovers plots are their catnip. They believe in three things-- the importance of representation, the awesomeness of Aquaman, and Buffy the Vampire Slayer. Their first novel Celebrity Spin Doctor was a double RITA award nominee.

OTHER BOOKS BY CELIA MULDER

The Celebrity Spin Doctor Series

Celebrity Spin Doctor

The Issue With Antons

Back On Top

Novellas

That Big Romantic Moment

Curses, Quests, and Cuties *in the anthology Magic &*
Mischief